# MOONE BOY

## THE BLUNDER YEARS

# Chris O'Dowd & Nick V. Murphy

# MOONE BOY

## THE BLUNDER YEARS

### ILLUSTRATED BY WALTER GIAMPAGLIA/CARTOON SALOON

MACMILLAN CHILDREN'S BOOKS

This edition published 2015 by Macmillan Children's Books
an imprint of Pan Macmillan
a division of Macmillan Publishers Limited
20 New Wharf Road, London N1 9RR
Associated companies throughout the world
www.panmacmillan.com

ISBN 978-1-4472-9320-0

135798642

A CIP catalogue record for this book is available from
the British Library.

Printed and bound by CPI Group (UK) Ltd, Croydon CR0 4YY

*To all the nieces and nephews and godchildren whose birthdays I always forget. This book is for you. Happy birthday. And to President Obama. He knows why.*

*Chris*


*To my three-year-old son, Leo, who insists I'm the funniest person he's ever met. May you never meet another person.*

*Nick*

Good afternoon, reader. Or good morning, listener. Or good evening, watcher, for those of you who are watching someone else read this novel and trying to guess the contents. Whoever you are, welcome to this book!

Before we begin, I need to carry out a quick survey.

Are you reading this book because:

A. You have a scientific interest in the moon.
B. You have a scientific interest in the misspelling of the word 'moon'.
C. You want to find out how quick and easy it is to obtain an imaginary friend that you'll cherish for life.
D. You'll read anything. You're just like that.

If your answer is A or B, then I'm afraid you're going to be disappointed. There's very little moon action in this story, apart from the brief appearance of a wrestler's wrinkly bum.

If your answer is C, then you'll be equally disappointed. I suggest you pick up a copy of *Imaginary Friends – The Quick and Easy Guide to Forever Friendship* by a former colleague of mine, Customer Service Representative 263748. He wrote it while working at the Corporate League of Imaginary Friends Federation. It's a comprehensive and well-researched body of work that will send you to sleep within seconds of opening its cover.

If your answer is D, then good for you! You're my kind of reader. I'm glad we got rid of that other bunch of idiots who picked A, B and C. And may I say, you're in for a treat. If you like shenanigans, you've come to the right book. These pages are riddled with ridicule, peppered with pranks and seasoned with spelling mistakes. So if you're looking for a tale that deals with the perils and hazards of imaginary friendship, you should find *Moone Boy: The Blunder Years* completely satisfactory.

So let's get on with it, my tea's getting cold. And stop picking your nose. You think I can't see you, but I can. And it's disgusting.

Anyway, enjoy the book. Just turn the page and proceed with Caution.

# CHAPTER ONE
# THE SCRUNCHIE INQUEST

> **Boyle, the third nipple of Ireland,**
> **on a wet Wednesday in the middle of the**
> **last month of the summer holidays.**
>
>  **Weather forecast: drizzle, with a**
> **chance of crizzle\* in the afternoon.**

It was the summer holidays, and it was raining. Again. Martin Moone might have been free from the shackles of the classroom, but now he was forced to do even more hard time at home, with the fierce females of his flippin' family. And he was fast finding out that women are a tricky bunch. Sisters are even trickier.

**\*CRIZZLE** – cloudy drizzle.

MOONE DICTIONARY

And *older* sisters have the ability to bewilder the finest magicians in the world with their tricksiness.

Martin Moone had three older sisters. And a very older mother, who was someone else's sister. This made the eleven-year-old simpleton feel like he was drowning in women. Or slowly submerging in female quicksand. Either way, not ideal.

If *only* his useless mother had given him a brother.

Just one.

Just a single tall, lanky companion to help him do battle with this legion of ladies.

But she hadn't. Probably just to spite him.

No, Martin Moone was alone in this fight. An army of one. And, on this wet Wednesday morning, as on every other morning, he found himself under siege.

'This was the best house in the world before you were born!' explained Sinead, jabbing a jammy finger at Martin's face. She then picked up her buttery toast and wrapped her snack-happy jaws around her sixth slice of the morning.

'Now, let's not go mad,' reasoned Martin. 'Sure, how could it have been the best house if I wasn't even in it?'

'That's why it was the best house in the world, ya plonk*!' repeated Sinead, spraying him with a mouthful of toast crumbs.

His other sisters, Fidelma and Trisha, murmured in agreement. They were eating breakfast while gawping at the television – clearly too busy to actually voice their dislike of their brother.

Martin had been accused of ruining his closest sister's scrunchie** by using it as a catapult. When I say 'closest', I mean in age. As siblings, they were as close to each other as a badger is to a trap.

*PLONK – another word for idiot. Named after the Irish order of PLaid mONKs, a check-shirt-wearing bunch of holy men, who were locally regarded as idiots.
**SCRUNCHIE – a simple rubber band, clothed in cotton, used by the long of hair to bunch their greasy, nit-infested manes into a manageable heap.

In Martin's defence, it must be said that a catapult is a device that requires a reasonable amount of upper-body strength. The amount of strength in Martin's upper body was very *unreasonable*. Pig-headed, even. Point being, there's no way this accusation could be true. His sisters' daily dead arms had surely made his insignificant little limbs far too weak to commit the crime. Pulling back the elasticated hairband and propelling a pebble skyward was clearly beyond his physical abilities. Case closed. An innocent man. Almost definitely.

But in the Moone kitchen, which this morning resembled a clan\* court, Martin was being subjected to quite the grilling.

'Better than the Taj Mahal?' asked Martin. It had only taken him three full minutes to

\*CLAN – Gaelic\*\* word for the fellow members of your personal human zoo, your family.
\*\*GAELIC – a lyrical and impossible language spoken in regions of Ireland, Scotland, Wales and, for some reason, France.

think of this smart-arse retort to Sinead's comment about their house.

'What are you talking about?' grunted Sinead, now horsing down a chocolate yogurt.

'You're saying that, before I was born, this . . . Irish igloo –' he pointed at various low points of the Moone kitchen to emphasize his point – 'this breezy bungalow, this mountain of mould, was better than say . . . the White House in America?'

He smirked, pleased with his joke and certain his quick wit would snip their sniping off at the knees.

'Are you being a clever-hole, Martin?' asked Trisha from the couch.

Martin glared at her. Trisha was the middle sister and so had been blessed with all the attributes saved for the average middle sister – a fear of being forgotten, which caused her to lash out, the ability to burn everything she cooked (even water) and, of course, a dislike or mistrust of all living things.

'He is and all,' hissed Sinead spitefully, as she sliced herself a wedge of old cheese that she'd found in the fridge. 'He's being a smart-hole.'

Fidelma looked up from her bowl of soggy ReadyBix*. 'Martin, just apologize and give Sinead your pocket money to buy a new scrunchie. Then we won't have to murder you and throw your body in the lake.'

'Who's goin' to the lake? I'll go to the lake if people are goin' to the lake.'

The children turned to find their father, Liam, standing in the kitchen doorway with a big happy head on him.

'I haven't been to the lake for ages,' he declared cheerfully.

Sinead and Martin began shouting again, each putting across their own case for their dad's judgement.

*READYBIX – a puddle of sawdust, oats and tears pretending to be breakfast cereal.

'Martin used my scrunchie as a catapult,' Sinead snorted, holding up the red sagging scrunchie like a murder weapon, 'and now it's too baggy!'

'What?! As if I could even use a catapult after all the dead arms you've given me!' Martin retorted. 'It's a miracle I can even feed myself!'

'Whoa, whoa, whoa!' groaned their clueless father. 'All right, calm down, speak one at a time or nobody's goin' to the lake.'

'Nobody *is* going to the lake, Dad!' they both blurted back at him.

'Well, not now they're not,' Liam insisted, putting his silly old foot down.

Fidelma and Trisha rolled their eyes and turned back to the flickering television screen.

'He's always using my stuff, Dad,' Sinead persevered. 'Last week he used my tights to catch worms.'

'They were attracted to your scent!' Martin explained.

'He broke a leg off my Sindy doll—'

'My Action Man prefers his damsels to be *really* distressed.'

'And he's always hogging my Fashion Wheel*.'

They all looked to Martin for an explanation. Martin cleared his throat as he searched for a reason why he had been using this oh-so-feminine crafting device. But all that came to him was:

'That's just an excellent toy.'

'Martin, did you use your sister's scrunchie as a catapult?'

'It hurts me that you even have to ask, Dad,' replied the mini-Moone.

Just then, Liam's inquisition of Martin was interrupted by the arrival of Mammy Moone.

'Has anyone seen my leather belt?'

*FASHION WHEEL – a common Christmas present in 1987. A plastic contraption for drawing and colouring lovely patterned dresses. Popular with girls, and their brothers when no one was looking.

she asked, as she rushed through the kitchen looking like a turbaned Margaret Thatcher*, her recently washed hair wrapped high in a towel. Debra Moone had a habit of rushing into and out of rooms, as mothers often do, which made Martin suspect that she had a secret identity far beyond the simple, lazy life she led as their mother.

'The green one?' asked Fidelma, the most likely belt-borrower in Boyle.

'No, no, my new one, the black leather one. Flippin' heck, can't keep a hold of anything in this house,' Debra complained as she exited the kitchen at speed, off to her war-room meeting or whatever.

'Dad, it's just not fair,' Sinead whined, still on the hunt for scrunchie retribution.

'Life isn't fair, love,' mused Liam, trying to be poetic.

*MARGARET THATCHER – the eldest and wartiest of the witches from Roald Dahl's wonderful book.

'Wise words, old man, I think we can all learn from that,' nodded Martin, tapping his father on the elbow appreciatively.

Sinead rolled her eyes as their mam rushed back in, her damp, limp hair now straddling her shoulders like the legs of a sick horse.

'What are they fighting about this time?' she asked her husband, patting her wet hair dry with an even wetter towel.

Liam, still pretending to focus on the conflict, whispered back, 'Who cares? I just use "life isn't fair" as my position on everything now.'

The slightest hint of an impressed smile from her mam was all that Sinead needed to go back on the attack.

'Martin used my scrunchie as a catapult and now it's ruined,' she squawked.

'I swear on my grave that's not true,' Martin offered, hand on heart.

'You don't have a grave, pal,' said Liam, sipping his tea.

'Then I swear on your grave, Dad.'

'We're all alive, Martin,' his mother reminded him.

'For now we are . . .' whispered Sinead, staring daggers at Martin. 'I'm gonna end you, ya flute*.'

'But I've only just begun!' Martin protested.

'Martin, did you or did you not use Sinead's scrunchie as a catapult?' Debra asked calmly and ominously.

'Absolutely not. And I'm growing tired of all these baseless accusations.'

'Did you use it for anything else?' added Mammy Moone, with a knowing look.

The room fell silent as all eyes turned to Martin.

'Well . . .'

'Did I see you practising karate in the garden this morning, Martin?' probed his mother,

*FLUTE – a melodic woodwind instrument. Also used as a personal insult, probably because it's such a pain in the bum to learn.

15

clearly ahead of the game.

'I may have been honing some of my moves, yes,' the boy offered sheepishly*.

'And were you pretending to be the Karate Kid by wearing Sinead's scrunchie as a headband, by any chance?' Debra quizzed, promptly wrapping up the case.

As Sinead and the girls gawped, Martin cleared his throat to make his final plea.

'It's the headband that makes it macho, Mam.'

As his sisters lobbed abuse at him, Martin's punishment came quickly.

'Buy Sinead a new scrunchie and stop stealing our flippin' stuff,' Debra ordered as she rushed off to meet some astronauts or whatever.

'Wait,' piped up Trisha, sensing blood.

*SHEEPISHLY - a long word for shy. Comes from the sheep world's lack of good public speakers.

16

'Wasn't the Karate Kid a *black belt*?'

Martin's head drooped as Debra spun on her heels and looked from her sagging belt loops to her flagging fruit loop of a son. She waited for an explanation. And waited.

Martin simply shrugged. 'A basic grasp of self-defence is very important in this house.'

A vicious dead arm from Sinead provided a fitting full stop to his point.

Martin was sick and tired of being terrorized by these turbulent teens. I can't fly this boy jet alone any more, he thought to himself. I need a co-pilot.

## CHAPTER TWO
## WHAT IF WHAT?

The next day, Martin explained his problem to his best friend, Padraic, who scrunched up his face, confused by it all. Padraic had a perfectly round face, like a pleasant dinner plate, or a tractor tyre, so it took a lot of confusion to scrunch it up.

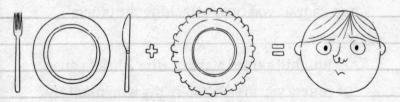

'So you're saying you need a male companion?'

'I am,' Martin nodded. 'It's the one thing I really need. Well, that, and maybe some kind of protective arm armour,' he added, rubbing the bruise where Sinead had thumped him.

'But don't you already *have* a male companion?'

'Who's that?' asked Martin blankly.

'Well – me.' Padraic wiped a splash of milk from the tip of his pudgy nose. 'Aren't *I* your male companion?'

The boys were standing in the cowshed of a large farm where Padraic was milking the cattle. A few of the big beasts were already hooked up to the noisy milking machine, having their daily dairy donation sucked out of them, and Padraic was busy attaching the others' udders.

'Riiight!' agreed Martin, after a brief pause. 'Of course you are, P! You're my wingman! My sidekick! My trusty steed!'

Padraic gave a delighted but slightly confused smile, and returned to his work.

'It's just . . .' Martin continued hesitantly, 'I was kinda thinking that, as well as your top-notch wingman-ship, I could also do with *another* wingman. A spare wingman. I mean . . . what's a plane with just one wing?'

'In trouble?' suggested Padraic, poking his head out from behind a big bovine's* bottom.

'Exactamundo, P-Dog – BIG trouble,' agreed Martin. 'The good ship Moone will crash-land pretty quickly if it has only one wing, especially when that wing has to milk cows all day long.'

Padraic stood up, looking a little hurt. 'Ah, Martin, you know Daddy needs help on the farm. And since I can't help during school-time, it's only fair that every summer he gets to work me like a dog.'

'He sure does. You're like a big, cow-milking dog.'

'That's exactly what I am.' Padraic nodded glumly.

*BOVINE – a fancy term for cow. Other fancy terms for cow include Lady Daisalot and the Duke of Bullshire.

'Hey, maybe that's the solution!' exclaimed Martin, brightening. 'Could you get a cow-milking dog?'

'Believe me, I've tried,' stated Padraic, turning to a sheepish-looking sheepdog sitting in the corner of the milking shed. 'Ya useless yoke\*!' he yelled, and the dog hung its head in shame.

'But hey,' he said, turning back to Martin, 'it's not that bad really. They may not look it, but these big beauties are a lot of craic\*\*.' He slapped a heifer's bum and she gave a loud fart in return.

Padraic laughed, delighted. 'Ha ha! See what I mean? Good old Windy Wendy!'

Martin was hit by a powerful stench and took a step back.

\*YOKE – a thing. Not the thing inside an egg though. That yoke is called a yolk.

\*\*CRAIC – pronounced 'crack'. The Irish word for fun. Although no one seems to know for sure what it means, as a lot of conversations in Ireland start with the question 'What's the craic?'

'And sure, whenever I need something more,' Padraic went on, 'I just turn to my good old IF.'

Martin gave a confused look as Padraic resumed his work.

'If?' he asked.

'What?'

'What if?'

'What if what?'

'What's a "good old if"?'

'Oh, that's just what I call them.'

'Call who?' asked Martin.

'Imaginary friends,' explained Padraic, with a shrug.

He made this comment as casually as could be, but until this moment Martin had been completely unaware that his best friend possessed an imaginary pal. Sure, he'd noticed Padraic murmur to himself on occasion, or giggle at an unheard joke, or even give a celebratory high five to no one in particular. But he'd never suspected that Padraic had the creative smarts to actually conjure up a fully formed friend.

Martin couldn't help feeling a slight pang of jealousy. It was like he'd just discovered that Padraic was in a gang that Martin wasn't part of. Although, in truth, Padraic was in *several* gangs that Martin wasn't part of:

- The Just Outside Boylers – a group of rural lads who got together once a month to wrestle in a field, trade jumpers with each other and complain about the Boyle 'townies*'.
- The Motley Maritimers – a barbershop quintet who specialized in sad sea shanties.
- The Knicker Knitters. For lovers of itchy undies.

*TOWNIES – a term for people in Ireland who live more than a stone's throw from a cowpat.

- The Fast and Furious Farmers – a gang of late-night drag-racing tractor drivers.
- And of course His Mother's Book Club – a gang that was so rife with division that they hadn't even agreed on a name, let alone a book to read.

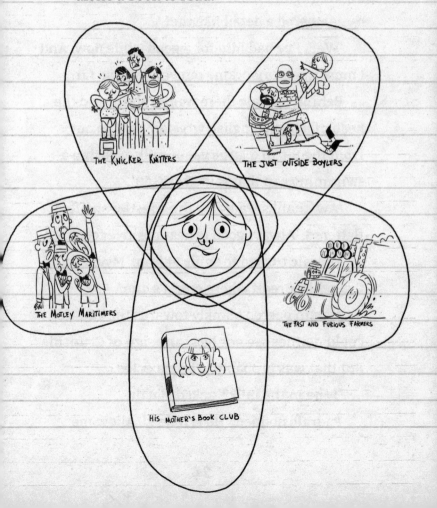

THE KNICKER KNITTERS

THE JUST OUTSIDE BOYLERS

THE MOTLEY MARITIMERS

THE FAST AND FURIOUS FARMERS

HIS MOTHER'S BOOK CLUB

'You've got an imaginary friend?' asked Martin.

'Well, yeah,' said Padraic. 'Did I never mention that?'

'No, you didn't!'

'Are you sure?'

'Yeah, I'm pretty sure I would have remembered a detail like that.'

'Well, I've had him for a good while now. And I must say he's working out very well so far.'

Behind Padraic there was a splash, and the head of a burly English wrestler peeked out from the top of a large vat of milk, wearing a swimming cap that said 'DANGER'.

'Aw, thanks, Padraic,' the wrestler sniffled, flattered. 'Always good to hear positive feedback.'

Padraic turned to smile at him. 'My pleasure, Crunchie. Credit where credit's due.'

Martin peered blankly towards the vat. He could neither see nor hear any sign of Crunchie. But that was probably to be expected.

'Is he in the milk?' asked Martin.

Padraic nodded. 'He is indeed. Allow me

to present Crunchie Haystacks. Middle name: Danger.'

'Danger!' yelled Crunchie, splashing around in the milk. 'Mmm, it's all warm and milky in here.'

'Well, that's cos it's warm milk,' Padraic explained. 'You're wearing a bathing suit though – right?' he asked, suddenly concerned.

Crunchie paused. 'Er . . . I'm wearing my birthday suit?'

'Aw, Crunchie, I told ya not to skinny-dip in the milk! It's unsanitary!'

'What's unsanitary about it? I'm wearing a swimming cap!' the wrestler yelled, and dived down into the milk, rearing his ruddy rear end into the air.

Padraic shook his head, chuckling. 'Ah, he's a gas* fella.'

*GAS – another word Irish people use for fun. It's said that the Eskimos have twenty-seven different words for snow. It's the same with the Irish and fun. And we're both freezing most of the time, so maybe that makes us smarter. Who knows?

'Is he in the nip?' asked Martin.

'He is, yeah.' Padraic nodded. 'To be honest, he's probably a little drunk, since it's after lunchtime. He's not exactly the most professional of IFs, but he is great craic. You should really think about getting one yourself.'

'An imaginary friend?'

'Why not? They're very cheap to feed. All I have to do is imagine Crunchie a bowl of Ready-bix every now and then and he's happy as a clam.'

'Right,' said Martin, then frowned. 'But you know the way you're talking away to him, and other people can't see him – don't you find that people think you're a little bit mental?'

'Ah yeah, that does come up every now and then. But it's a small price to pay. Right, Crunchie?' said Padraic, looking across the room.

'I thought he was in the vat,' said Martin.

'No, he's towelling off now.'

'My fingers were starting to curdle,' confessed Crunchie, as he draped a towel over his head like a soggy sultan. 'Ya know,

I could refer your pal to a few colleagues if he wants,' he suggested to Padraic. 'Hamish the Headbutter is looking for work these days. And Pile-Driver Pete's been unemployed since he knocked his realsie* out by mistake.'

'Aw, that's very decent of you, Crunchie,' Padraic commented.

'What's that now?' asked Martin.

'Crunchie said he could hook you up with one of the wrestling IFs if you want. Make a few introductions.'

Martin looked around. 'Oh. Er, thanks, Crunchie.'

'He's over here now,' said Padraic, gesturing beside him.

Martin turned back to them. 'But if I was to get an IF, I'm not sure I'd be looking for a wrestling IF.'

'Suit yourself.' Padraic shrugged. 'But you don't know what you're missing!'

*REALSIE – a non-imaginary. Someone you can poke.

And with that, he suddenly pounced on Crunchie and put him into a headlock. 'Gotcha, ya big milky meatball!'

'Agh! No fair!' yelled Crunchie as he staggered around, trying to get free. 'What happened to three-second warnings!?'

'I make the rules, tubby! Say, "Mercy!"'

'Never!'

'Say, "Mercy," or I'll clothesline* you! Ya big English eejit**!'

Martin took a couple of steps back, deciding it was probably time to be going. 'Right so,' he said, 'well, I'll leave you lads to it.'

'Bye, Martin!' Padraic waved, struggling to keep a grip on Crunchie.

Martin waved goodbye and headed off, leaving Padraic in the cowshed, wrestling himself.

*CLOTHESLINE – a wrestling move where the wrestler pretends to be a clothesline. It's a lot more violent than it sounds.
**EEJIT – yet another word for idiot. Used because it sounds like someone trying to say 'idiot' after they've stupidly got their tongue stuck to an ice cube.

# CHAPTER THREE
## IF I HAD AN IF MAN

That night Martin lay awake in his bed, unable to sleep. Most people would have assumed that this was due to the great honking snores that were coming from Sinead's bed across the room – a noise that sounded like a wild boar snuffling for truffles* in a deep swamp of wet snot. And they wouldn't have been far wrong. But that wasn't the only reason he was wide awake.

Martin just couldn't stop thinking about what Padraic had told him. And the more he thought about it, the more he started to like the idea of an imaginary friend.

*TRUFFLES – not, as you'd expect, the delicious balls of chocolate, but some kind of fungus that rich people put in pasta. Rich people are very odd. Personally I can't eat pasta without chocolate.

'An IF,' he said to himself quietly, 'An
IF could be just the thing. My own personal
dancing monkey! Life would be a whole lot
more fun if I had an IF man.'

He grinned at this thought and began
humming a tune from a film he'd once seen
about a rooftop fiddler, although he couldn't
remember the name of it.

He sang softly to himself:

If I had an IF man,
Ya ba dibba dibba dibba dibba dibba dibba
    dum,
All day long I'd biddy biddy bum,
If I had a little IFfy man.

I could get a tall one,
A fatty or a beardy or a teeny tiny elf,
I could be singing to him now,
Instead of to my boring old self.

*I wouldn't have to think hard,*
*He'd have to entertain me and we'd have a*
   *lot of fun,*
*Two lads against the world,*
*And two is nearly twice as good as one.*

Martin stopped singing and sat up in bed. It was decided. And like all his best decisions, it had been decided through song.

'OK, Imaginary Friend,' he said. 'Begin!'

He stared into the darkness expectantly, but nothing happened.

Not really sure what else to do, he clapped his hands once, hoping that this would start the process. But still nothing happened.

'I said, begin!' Martin ordered, more loudly this time.

Across the room Sinead grunted, and the snoring paused for a moment.

'Begin what?' she yelled at him.

'Er, nothing,' said Martin, and lay back down.

'Who were ya talking to?'

'No one.'

She snorted a laugh. 'Ya muppet*.'

A few moments later, the snoring resumed and Martin pondered silently to himself. Maybe this isn't going to be as easy as I thought, he thought. Maybe there's some special trick to getting an IF. Maybe I need to—

'I said, shut up!' barked Sinead.

'I wasn't saying anything,' protested Martin.

'I can hear ya thinking, ya big thinking spanner**!'

Martin sighed and tried to stop using his brain. He just lay there, staring at the ceiling, trying to empty his head of all thoughts – which was actually a lot easier than expected. Soon his empty head was fast asleep, lost in dreams about absolutely nothing.

*MUPPET – famous puppets. A group of cheeky American megastars who stole the thunder from Punch and Judy.

**SPANNER – a wrenching tool that idiots often try to use as a hammer.

# CHAPTER FOUR
## HOW, WHY AND WHERE
## TO GET AN IF

'So, how *do* you get an IF?' Martin asked Padraic the next day. 'Is there some sort of trick to it? Cos I already tried clapping and that didn't work.'

'Ah yeah.' Padraic nodded. 'Clapping won't do it. Clapping might get you some kind of a genie or something, but it won't get you an IF.'

'So what's your technique?' asked Martin, clicking the end of his pen. He had a copybook open on his lap and was poised, ready to take notes. 'Tell me everything, P-Bomb. I'm all ears.'

Padraic sat back and gazed thoughtfully through the windshield of his combine harvester*. He was sitting at the enormous

*COMBINE HARVESTER – a machine that harvests grain crops, like wheat and barley. Common brands of combine harvester include John Deere, Massey Ferguson, Tony Ferino and Sassy McDuff.

steering wheel and Martin was perched beside him, a bit squished against the door. They were surrounded by a field of tall wheat that Padraic was halfway through harvesting. Right now he was on his tea break, and the massive machine sat silent as Padraic munched his last custard-cream biscuit and washed it down with a mouthful of milky tea. He wiped his mouth with the sleeve of his shirt and went back to gazing pensively out at the land.

'Before I tell you, Martin,' he said, in a slightly mysterious voice, 'are you sure you want to go down this road?'

'Well, you're the one who suggested it,' said Martin with a shrug.

Padraic nodded slowly and continued to stare into the middle distance. 'I just want you to be sure, Martin. Cos this road is a dangerous one. A bumpy, dangerous, bumpy road. With twists and turns and twists and great big potholes. And lots of litter scattered along the sides.'

'You mean, like the road to your house?'

'Yes. It's very much like the road to our house,' agreed Padraic. 'Except this road doesn't go to our house. No, sir.'

'Where *does* it go?'

Padraic turned to face him. 'That's what you've got to find out, Martin.'

Martin nodded slowly, pondering this, and pretended to write it down. In fact he had no clue what Padraic was talking about and was drawing a little doodle instead.

'Many have tried to get an IF before you,' Padraic went on, 'and many have failed.'

'Really? Who?'

Padraic paused for a moment. 'Actually, no, I don't think anyone's failed.'

'So everyone who sets out to get an imaginary friend has got one?'

'Yes, I think there's basically a one-hundred-per-cent success rate at this.'

'Oh. That's good.'

'Yeah, that should be encouraging.'

'So how do I get started?' asked Martin. 'Is there a number to call? Or someone I need to bribe?'

'Well, to be honest,' said Padraic plainly, 'the simplest way to get an imaginary friend is just to imagine him.'

'Oh, I've tried that,' said Martin. 'But it doesn't seem to be working.'

Padraic nodded slowly, and then noticed Martin's doodle in the copybook. 'What's that you're drawing?'

'A picture of me,' said Martin with a shrug.

'Doing what?'

'Just standing there.'

Padraic studied the sketch for a moment, then looked at Martin. 'Your imagination really isn't the best, is it?'

'It's pathetic.' Martin nodded sadly. 'That's why I need an imaginary friend. To do the imagining for both of us.'

Padraic supped down the last of his tea and screwed the cap back on to his flask.

'Well, Martin, if you're not able to imagine an imaginary friend, then you should probably just order one from the catalogue.'

'There's a catalogue?' Martin exclaimed. 'Padraic, we've just had quite a long conversation about this, and only now do you mention that there's a catalogue! For future reference, always tell me first if there's a catalogue.'

Padraic shrugged. 'I like to keep you on your toes.'

Martin shook his head, a bit annoyed. 'So how do I get the flippin' catalogue then?'

'Right, yes. This is where it gets interesting. You need to take a stamped addressed envelope and bring it to the middle of Boyle Forest.'

Martin picked up his pen again. 'Right! Facts. Good. We're getting somewhere now. Boyle Forest. Then what?'

Padraic could see his father, Farmer O'Dwyer, making his way through the field towards them.

'Daddy's coming. Time to get back to work.'

'Not before you tell me what to do with the stamped addressed envelope!'

Padraic turned to him and spoke quickly now, urgency in his voice. 'You need to make your way to the west corner of the forest, where the nettles are at their thickest. You must walk through them and get stung seven times – no more, no less. Then crawl through a mile of thorny brambles until you reach the treacherous trail. Follow it to the deepest, darkest part of the forest. And once there, take your stamped addressed envelope and leave it inside the hollow of the Great Imaginary Tree.'

'The what?!' asked Martin, scribbling all this down.

Just then, the door was yanked open and Martin tumbled out on to the ground. Padraic's father peered down at him. He was a short, stocky farmer with a clean-shaven face and a wild head of red hair – if you were looking at him upside down, which Martin was. He righted himself, getting to his feet, and was then looking at a bald man with a wild red beard.

Farmer O'Dwyer turned to his son. 'Tea break's over, Padraic,' he mumbled. 'This field isn't going to harvest itself. Unless you've

planted self-harvesting grain. Did you plant
self-harvesting grain?'

'No, Daddy.'

'Why not?'

'Because . . . there's no such thing?'

'Exactly, Padraic. There's no such thing as
self-harvesting grain.'

'Sorry, Daddy.'

Martin gave him a friendly wave. 'Hi, Farmer
O'Dwyer!'

Padraic's father looked from Martin to
Padraic. 'Who's this clown?'

'My best friend, Martin,' said Padraic.

There was a pause as Farmer O'Dwyer
showed no sign of recognition.

'Moone,' Padraic added.

'We've met before,' said Martin brightly.

Farmer O'Dwyer peered at him suspiciously.
'Is that right?'

'Er. Yeah,' said Martin, a little confused.
'Many times. At birthday parties. And
sleepovers. And general calling over.'

Farmer O'Dwyer continued to stare at him blankly. 'Did you used to have a moustache?'

'Ahm. I don't think so, Farmer O'Dwyer,' answered a confused Martin.

'Then I don't know you. Are ya going to help Padraic harvest the field?' he grunted.

'Oh, that'd be great, Martin!' said Padraic, perking up. 'It'd be lovely to have some human company for once!'

'Ehh . . .' said Martin vaguely, glancing at his watch. 'Well, the thing is, *MacGyver** is on in ten minutes, so I really need to be shooting off.'

Padraic sagged back in his seat, disappointed.

'Right so,' grunted Padraic's dad. He touched one of his nostrils and gave a loud snort, sucking up his snot. 'Back to work, Padraic,'

*MACGYVER* – a TV show from the 1980s where a man could make any number of incredibly useful things out of whatever fluff he found in his belly button.

he said, then hocked and spat on the ground.

He winked at Martin. 'Good to meet ya, Marvin.' Then strolled off in his mucky wellies.

Padraic gave Martin an apologetic look. 'Sorry, pal. He's not great with faces. Or names. Or any combination of the two.'

Martin opened his copybook and checked his notes. 'Right. So I head for the nettles, seven stings, then brambles, treacherous trail, deepest part of the forest, find the Imaginary Tree and stuff the envelope inside it. Is that it?'

'That's it, yeah.'

'This journey sounds like a real pain in the backside.'

'Well, if your prefer, you *could* just take the path.'

'What path?'

'The primrose path. It's probably an easier route. And the smell is divine.'

Martin shook his head wearily and ripped the page out of his copybook, crumpling it up. 'Always tell me first if there's a path!'

Padraic shrugged apologetically as he started up the engine. 'I'm allergic to primroses, so I prefer the treacherous way.'

'Hey, one more thing,' Martin said, turning back to Padraic. 'How will I know if I've found the right tree?'

'Oh, you'll know the Imaginary Tree when you see it,' Padraic assured him with a smile.

'How?'

'Because the Imaginary Tree will be the only one that's not there!' yelled Padraic, as he headed off through the wheat field on his metal beast.

Martin nodded, thinking about this. 'Makes sense,' he said, and strolled off for home.

# CHAPTER FIVE
## THREE FOR A GIRL,
## FOUR FOR A BOY

Martin went to bed that night as giddy as a
shepherd. He was so excited by the prospect of
his new life as an IF owner, he decided to rise at
the break of dawn the next morning and head
out to the forest. But alas, Martin was a heavy
sleeper and lazy as a shepherd. So as noon hit
the Moone house, Martin sloped
out of his leaba* and made his
way to the back door with
some burnt toast in his gob.

'Where are you off to,
Martin?' his mother asked,

*LEABA – the Irish word for bed. This
is where 'the magic happens' – if you
believe dreams are magic. I believe they're
witchcraft, but then all my dreams do
involve bats in hats.

as she rushed around trying to make herself look busy.

'Oh . . . I'm just . . . heading off to . . . Ahm . . .' Martin struggled to think on his feet at the best of times, and at the worst of times he struggled to think sitting down. 'Just . . . heading off to . . . bury . . . my . . . my . . . camel . . . in the . . . hedge . . . hog.' He winced at his own stupidity.

'Did you brush your teeth?' asked his mother, clearly not listening, as she slid from counter to counter, bringing a dishcloth with her without ever using it.

'Ahm . . . No, my toothbrush . . . ahm . . . fell on to the . . . the ceiling.' He shook his head at himself.

'All right, see ya later so,' replied Debra as she rushed off to not use her dishcloth in another room.

Nailed it, Martin thought to himself, as he high-fived his own hand and slipped out the back door.

Boyle Forest was around five miles from the Moone house. So on a decent bicycle it was just a half-hour ride along a pleasant country road.

Unfortunately Martin didn't have a decent bicycle. He had a terribly *in*decent bicycle in fact. The kind of rusty vehicle that creaked and squeaked with every turn of the pedals, making the rider sound like a flatulent* ferret. It was also a girls' bike.

It used to be Sinead's bike. Before that it was Trisha's, and before THAT it was Fidelma's. But now it was Martin's. It was pink and brown. Well, reddish brown. All right, rusty brown. It was basically just rust. It was pink and rust. There were ribbons glued to the mudguards of the front wheel, which would whip Martin's chin when the wind caught them. For some reason, a single training wheel remained

*FLATULENT* – a pleasant term for farting. Like windypops. Or bum breeze.

doggedly attached at the back. This lonesome wheel always reminded Martin of his transition from boy to youth. It also reminded him of how useless his father was with a spanner.

As with all ladies' bikes, there was no crossbar, which never made sense to Martin. He was no doctor, he was barely a nurse, but even he knew that if a fella fell on to a crossbar then surely it would do more damage than if a lady did.

He tried not to think about that right now because he really was at his worst if he was forced to think while pedalling.

Finally there was a crusty bell on the handlebars, which clunked rather than rang, to let people know that an idiot was coming.

An hour later, having been subjected to taunts, insults and a surprising number of wolf-whistles* from passers-by, Martin arrived at Boyle Forest on his ladies' bike.

He pulled the stamped addressed envelope from his jacket pocket, discarded his rusty fart generator in a bush and made his way to the west corner of the forest.

Padraic was right, the nettles here were very thick, and as he counted their bitter stings – 'One . . . Two . . . *ow*, that was a big one,

*WOLF-WHISTLE – the sort of whistle that means, 'Hey, good lookin'!' This is why wolves have a reputation for being very complimentary.

three . . . four . . . flippin' heck that's sore . . .' –
he suddenly recalled something he'd forgotten
to remember. What was it? . . . Ah, can't be
more important than this, he thought, as he
reached out to self-sting himself again. 'Five . . .
six . . . Wait a blinkin' minute!'

A little later he was on the primrose path,
nursing his nettle-bitten hands with a dock leaf.
He'd have been more annoyed with himself, but
the sweet-smelling primroses had put a spring
in his step.

How could Padraic be allergic to these
delicate flowers? Real men should only be
allergic to dangerous things.

THINGS I'M ALLERGIC TO:

- STRAWBERRIES
- SILK
- SHARKS
- SUDS

THAT'S ALL. THAT'S ALL THE THINGS THAT
I'M ALLERGIC TO. THAT BEGIN WITH THE
LETTER S.

MOVING ON TO THE LETTER T...

- THIMBLES
- TREACLE
- TUMBLEWEED
- TURTLES
- TINSEL
- TOMCATS
- THUMBTACKS
- TURPENTINE
- TUNA FISH
- TUPPERWARE
- TRANQUILLIZERS (HORSE)
- TAMBOURINES
- TWEEZERS

PTO

When he reached the end of the primrose path, Martin found himself in the middle of the wood. And what a woody wood it was. There were ferns and oaks and . . . other trees Martin could have named if he'd ever listened in nature class.

He made his way through the thick forest undergrowth, tiptoeing quietly and carefully. There was no real reason to do this, but he liked to make things feel more exciting for the craic.

He spotted a clearing in the distance, where no trees grew. Ah, he thought to himself, here we go. He actually said, 'Here we go', out loud, even though he'd just meant to think it, which gave him a hop*.

As he approached the clearing, something very odd happened.

A magnificent magpie swooped down and sat in the centre of the shadowed circle.

Martin made eye contact with it. The big bird returned his gaze. And before long, Martin realized he was having a staring contest with a magpie. It went on for quite a while. Then he remembered something his mother always

*HOP – a slight startle. A surprise that makes only one of your legs jump.

did whenever she encountered a magpie. A 'salutation', she called it.

'Good morning, Mr Magpie, how's your wife?' offered Martin, a bit embarrassed, but hoping his greeting would end the eye-lock deadlock.

'Grand, thanks. Bit of flu, but then there's always something wrong with her,' replied the magpie. 'Um, I couldn't help but notice you were staring at me there,' the bird added awkwardly.

'Oh,' said Martin. 'I thought we were having a staring contest.'

'Oh, right. No, that'd be weird. I was just looking at the trees and stuff.'

Martin looked embarrassed and tried to think of something witty to break the ice, but as per usual, nothing came.

'Anyway, I'd better get some Lemsip for her indoors before she shouts the nest down. See ya.' And with that, the magpie flapped his feathers and headed skyward.

'Bye now . . .' offered Martin. As he watched the bird take off, he couldn't help but notice it leaving a little present behind. When the magpie was a few feet off the ground, it did a tiny poo. As Martin watched the farewell plop hit the ground, he saw it grow. And grow and grow and grow. It got higher and higher, until branches developed, twigs twigged and leaves leafed.

It was a tree!

In the middle of its giant trunk, a big gnarly, knotted nose seemed to appear. And below that, a quite delicate little mouth. If Martin's knowledge of nature was as good as he thought it was, this sycamore tree had a face.

'I'm a spruce,' said Bruce.

# CHAPTER SIX
# THE GREAT IMAGINARY TREE

'I mean, jus' look at my tin bristles and my slim trunk,' said Bruce the Spruce in what sounded like a strong Scandinavian* accent. 'You tink a sycamore could pull off dis posture?'

'Sorry,' said Martin. 'I usually use nature class as my post-tea-break nap time.'

'Jis is stoopid excuse, but you say sorry, so I forgive,' replied the kind tree.

'A spruce, you say? That rings a bell. Like a Norwegian spruce?' asked Martin tentatively.

'No Norwegian, I'm the Dutch.'

*SCANDINAVIAN - person from northern Europe. In Viking times their strong men flattened armies and conquered countries. These days they flatten Ikea furniture and conquer cluttered bedrooms with handy storage units.

'Like a Dutch elm?' suggested Martin, unsure.

'No Elm, a Spruce, stoopid! We not all come from one place or anover, Martin, don't be a tree racist!'

Martin had never been accused of being a tree racist before. But then, it's likely that nobody had ever been accused of being a tree racist before. So he didn't mind.

'I'm sorry, Mr Spruce. I didn't mean to—'

'Bruce!' snapped the tree in reply.

'I'm sorry, Mr Bruce.'

'No, my name is Bruce. I Bruce de Spruce.'

'Oh, well, that's easy to remember,' Martin said, as he wrote down the name on his hand to help remember it. 'Sorry about the confusion.'

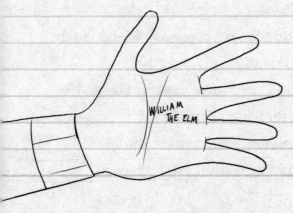

'Dis is OK, Martin. We got off on da bad foot, but we friends now.'

'Thank you. Listen, I should probably ask . . .' Martin started, even though he should really have known the answer, considering he was engaging with a talking Dutch Spruce that had grown from a magpie's poo, 'are you the Imaginary Tree?'

'Yesh!' confirmed the enthusiastic evergreen. 'Let me guesh, you be looking for a flying carpet, yesh?'

'No,' said Martin.

'De password to pass de troll bridge?'

'No, but let's come back to that one,' replied the boy.

'So what ish it you want, Martin?' asked Bruce, confused.

'I'm looking for an imaginary friend,' said Martin, confidently.

'Ahhhhh . . . Of course you are. You no like haff to tink for yourself, yesh?'

'Exactamundo, Mister Bruce, the less thinking I have to do the better, I reckon.'

'Okely-dokely. You have de shtamp addresh envelope?' asked Bruce, as he put on some reading glasses.

'Indeed I do, sir,' replied Martin, pulling it out of his pocket like a golden ticket.

Martin approached the great tree and looked around for somewhere to deposit the envelope. There was a small nook a foot below Bruce's dainty little mouth, and Martin started to stuff it in.

'My flippin neck!' squealed Bruce, taken aback. 'You trying to decapitate me, Martin?'

'God, no, no! I'm so sorry.'

'Hahahahaha . . . I joke, that ish de right place, you stoopid.' Bruce laughed as he began examining the envelope. 'But . . . dis is the wrong shtamp.'

Martin looked confused and took the envelope back from the nook.

'De problem here is, you supposed to use a twenty-pence shtamp, and what you did is jus draw a picture of youself where de shtamp's meant to be.'

'I see,' said Martin. 'I suppose I thought . . .
because it's imaginary—'

'You suppose wrong,' interrupted Bruce. 'I
can't mail this, Pat be laughing at me.'

'Your postman is called Pat?' asked Martin.

'Post*woman*. She a very strict lady with quite
da vicious white-and-black dog.'

'Right,' Martin said, unsure of his next
move. 'Well, maybe just this once, she'll take
an envelope without a real shtamp – I mean,
stamp.'

'No,' said Bruce. 'Pat very clear about dis
nonsense. You need to go home, get real shtamp
and come back tomorrow.'

Martin sighed. 'You really want me to cycle home and get a flippin' stamp?' he asked as he looked at the envelope. No reply came. Martin looked up to plead with the Dutch dream wrecker, but the giant tree had disappeared.

So off he went, shaking his head in frustration. He made his way through the thick stinging nettles for quite a while before remembering the primrose path. He really was quite a simpleton.

Martin returned the following day, armed with a real stamp he'd nicked from some cheque his father had told him to post. After hearing of Mrs Magpie's bunions* and watching the transformation of the bird's turd, he once again came face to chin with his lean mean evergreen.

*BUNION – a disease of the foot. Mostly caused by eating other people's toenails. Eating your own toenails, however, is a harmless pursuit.

'A shtamp!' remarked the impressed tree.

'Yes, sir, freshly licked and ready to go,' said Martin, happy with himself as he posted the envelope again. 'So, bye then,' Martin waved, and headed off, eager to get home.

'Wait! I don't deal with dish. I jus check for the shtamp.'

Martin's head dropped as he turned, frustrated.

'So I came all the way back out here for nothing?' he said, tapping his wrist, as if he had a watch. 'You're not the one who gives out imaginary friends?'

'I check for da shtamp.' Bruce shrugged. 'You have shtamp, I done. Unless you want lottery tickets? I also sell lottery tickets.'

'What's the prize?' asked Martin, his interest piqued.

'Shtamps,' replied Bruce.

'Ya know . . . This whole set-up really needs some work,' Martin complained. 'It's confusing, it's riddled with riddles, there's a lot of nettle stinging. I'm a busy man. I'm on my summer holidays, I've spent four hours cycling back and forth on a bicycle that belongs on a bonfire and I'm still no closer to getting an imaginary friend. I'm flippin' furious!'

'You need to give the shtamp addresh envelope to Laurel the Laurel,' Bruce said.

'Laurel the Laurel?' Martin repeated. 'And where would one find her? On the creepy island full of wolves?! In the Sahara?! In Cork*?!'

'Howya,' came a soft but speedy male voice. 'Cork is brilliant, isn't it?'

Martin looked around for its source.

'Lotta people think Texas is bigger than Cork, but it isn't. I'm telling you,' added the breathless voice.

Martin looked high and low, left and right, and eventually noticed a large bush directly behind Bruce the Spruce.

'There's four zoos. And forty-eight car washes. I think that says it all really.'

---

*CORK – a county in Ireland where we send all the troublemakers. Like an Irish Texas. But everyone there thinks that Cork is bigger than Texas.

'Yeah,' said Martin. 'Cork is big.'

'You got that right, boy. I'm Laurel the Laurel. Who you be?'

'I . . . be Martin? Isn't Laurel a girl's name?'

'Wha!? No. It's a boy's name. What are you, some kinda tree sexist, is it?'

'No! I'm not a . . .'

'Bitta confusion with your shtamp, I heard, tree sexist.'

'All shorted now, Laurel,' said Bruce.

'Good stuff, hand her over now so, don't have all day.'

Martin, who'd only just got used to Bruce's weird accent was pretty thrown by this new voice. It sounded like a normal person who got excited as the end of a sentence approached. Like he was running out of breath for what he wanted to say. But also, smug.

He decided not to point this out, as he was still worried about appearing to be a tree racist or even a tree sexist, so he handed Laurel the Laurel his stamped addressed envelope and stepped back, twiddling his thumbs.

'This looks grand yeah,' said Laurel. 'Off ya pop so, and don't forget to tell everyone how brilliant Cork is.' He waved Martin off with a swish of his branch.

'Wait,' Martin said. 'What happens now?'

'The usual, boy.'

'But I've never done this before,' started Martin. 'What's the usual?'

'Genie mac*, these new fellas will be the death of me, Bruce,' complained Laurel. 'In the mornin' you'll receive an IF catalogue in the post. Circle your choice and bury it in the garden. Easy-peasy like. Then shout, "Cork is the best!" twenty times at the top of your voice and go back inside.'

'Twenty times?' Martin queried.

'Well, that last bit is optional,' Laurel said. 'Then wait a day or so, depending on

*GENIE MAC – Cork talk meaning 'flippin' heck!'. A Genie Mac is also a type of burger, like a Big Mac, but served in a lamp.

71

Postwoman Pat's mood like, and your IF will arrive in your wardrobe.'

This was a lot of information to take in, so Martin decided to write it down on his hand.

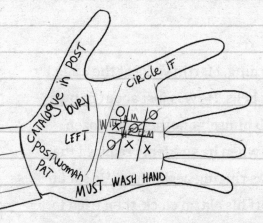

He also wrote 'Must wash hand' on his hand.

'Well, thanks for all your –' Martin looked up from his hand to thank the weird trees and saw that they'd both vanished. On the ground where Laurel had stood, he noticed that a small, light brown object remained. He walked over, tiptoeing quietly as he went (still making things exciting for himself) and picked it up. It was the top of a wine bottle.

Laurel had left a piece of Cork behind.

## CHAPTER SEVEN
## POSTWOMAN PAT

The next morning, Martin woke at the ungodly hour of eight bells. He was just about to turn over and grab himself another half-dozen bells of sleep when he suddenly realized that a loud bell was ringing beside him. He sat up and turned off his alarm clock, then tried to remember why he'd set it.

'The post!' he suddenly blurted out.

'*You're* a post*,' grunted Sinead in her sleep.

But Martin was already bounding out of bed with excitement. He hopped into his slippers, threw on his dressing gown and dashed down

*YOU'RE A POST – an Irish insult for someone who is as thick as a plank of wood or as lost as a piece of mail.

the hallway, giddy with anticipation.

At the front door, he scanned the mat. It was empty. Postwoman Pat had yet to make her delivery.

'Yes!' cried Martin. 'I haven't missed it!'

He then proceeded to wait there, staring at the letter box, like an eager but slightly dim-witted dog.

His father poked his head out from the kitchen, holding a cup of tea.

'You haven't missed what?'

Martin looked at him, startled. He'd assumed everyone else was asleep. After all, it was eight flippin' o'clock.

'What are you doing?' asked Liam.

'Nothing.' Martin shrugged. 'Just hangin' out.'

'In the hall?'

'Er, yeah. Sometimes I just hang out here.'

'Why?'

'I dunno.' Martin shrugged again, looking around the drab hallway, trying to think of a good reason. 'I suppose just cos we're always . . .

walking through here. But sometimes it's good to just . . . stop, you know? And take it in.'

Liam nodded thoughtfully. He stepped out into the hallway and looked around. 'I think I know what you mean, pal. Sometimes I like to get up early too, have a bit of "me-time". Make a cup of tea, sit in the kitchen and then sometimes I close my eyes and just imagine I'm the only one here. The only living soul in the whole house.'

Martin frowned slightly. 'Like we're all dead?'

'Ah no, no.' Liam chuckled. 'Nothing like that. Just like you're all . . . gone.'

'Gone where?'

'Oh, I don't know. Just . . . vanished,' he said cheerfully.

'Like we've been abducted by aliens?'

Liam laughed. 'Haha. Something like that.' He ruffled Martin's hair, smiling fondly. 'Well, I'll leave you to it, pal. Don't want to interrupt your me-time.'

He wandered off into the kitchen and Martin turned back to the letter box.

Still no post.

Any minute now! he thought to himself excitedly.

Three hours later, Martin was still waiting by the letter box, but he was now sprawled on the floor, fast asleep.

Trisha passed by, yawning, and trod on his leg.

'Ow!' yelped Martin, then sat up and looked at the mat. It remained stubbornly letter-less. 'Hey, Trisha, what time does the post come?'

'I dunno,' she grunted. 'Sometime in the morning?'

'What time is it now?'

She shrugged. 'Sometime in the morning?'

'Great stuff!' said Martin, hopping to his feet. 'Should be here any second!'

Trisha moved off into the kitchen as their mam looked out at her idiot son.

'Why are you waiting for the post, Martin?'

'Oh, er, no reason,' he answered coyly. 'But let's just say old Pat's got a special delivery with my name on it.'

Debra frowned. 'Our postman's name is Pat?'

Just then there was the sound of footsteps outside and a few envelopes began to poke through the letter box.

'At last!' Martin screeched, and yanked the door open.

A surprised-looking postman was crouched before him, trying to deliver their mail.

'Oh. Hello, Martin,' he said amiably.

Martin ripped the letters from his hand and flicked through them quickly.

The postie smiled at him and Debra. 'And how is the Moone family on this lovely—'

'Nothing but useless flippin' bills!' shouted Martin.

He threw them on the floor in frustration and stormed back to his room.

'Martin!' yelled his mam, but he was gone.

She turned back to the postman, embarrassed. 'Sorry about that, Pat.'

He frowned, a bit taken aback. 'Er. My name's not Pat, Debra.'

'Oh. Sorry. I thought, er . . .'

'I've been your postman for seventeen years. All this time you thought my name was "Postman Pat"?'

'No!' said Debra, getting flustered. 'Sorry. Postman . . . ?'

'It's Matt.'

'Matt.' Debra nodded, looking mortified. 'Sorry about that, Postman Matt.'

The man walked off, looking disgusted.

Debra shut the door, then yelled down the hallway,

'Martin! Why did you tell me his name was Pat?'

'Cos that's what the flippin' laurel bush told me!' Martin called back.

Debra shook her head in bewilderment and returned to the kitchen.

79

Back in his bedroom, an annoyed Martin was throwing a right strop*.

'It's all just a sack of nonsense!' he yelled, and flung a coat on the floor in anger.

He paced around the room, mumbling to himself furiously. 'Imaginary Trees. Talking magpies. Stupid stamped addressed envelopes. What a bunch of bullroar**!'

He kicked his wardrobe in frustration, and the wooden door creaked open. He gave it another hard slam, but the door bounced back, opening wider.

'Stupid door!'

He was just about to slam it again when suddenly he saw something lying at the bottom

*STROP – a tantrum for those above the age of a toddler. The quieter form is a 'huff', which becomes a 'strop' once a coat is flung on the floor.
**BULLROAR – silly nonsense. Like the notion of a bull roaring. As we all know, bulls only ever huff, snort or yodel.

of his wardrobe. Martin's eyes widened with astonishment as he gazed at the same stamped addressed envelope that he'd stuffed inside the Imaginary Tree the day before.

He knelt down and seized it with both hands. He ripped it open as quickly as he could and yanked out its precious contents. He tossed aside the envelope and then gave a gleeful grin as he finally laid eyes on the glossy, glorious catalogue.

A CLIFF Publication

# WHIF?

## Which IF?

INSIDE :

IFFY AWARD
NOMINATIONS
ANNOUNCED

-Special offers on bilingual IFs.
-New coupons for IF accessories!

# CHAPTER EIGHT
## THE CATALOGUE

Martin spent most of that day in his bedroom reading the catalogue. It was a shiny, expensive-looking magazine called *WhIF?*, which suggested something stinky but was actually just short for 'Which IF?'. It was filled with glossy pictures of every kind of imaginary friend, along with pages of assorted advertisements – for imaginary hats, imaginary banks, imaginary aftershave, even imaginary underwear.

There were about a hundred profiles of imaginary friends who were all available for work. They were an intriguing bunch, ranging from giant rabbits to robots, pixies to pirates, superheroes to scientists, and trapeze artists to con artists. There was even a Pope, a giant slug

and a reverse-mermaid*. There were pictures
of dancing IFs, foreign-language IFs, nerdy IFs,
obese IFs, scary IFs, smiley Ifs and of course
wrestling IFs.

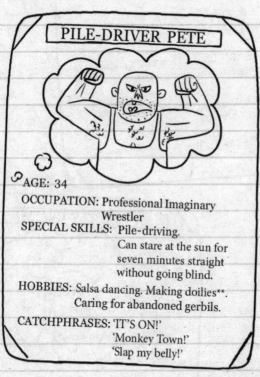

PILE-DRIVER PETE

AGE: 34
OCCUPATION: Professional Imaginary
Wrestler
SPECIAL SKILLS: Pile-driving.
Can stare at the sun for
seven minutes straight
without going blind.
HOBBIES: Salsa dancing. Making doilies**.
Caring for abandoned gerbils.
CATCHPHRASES: 'IT'S ON!'
'Monkey Town!'
'Slap my belly!'

*REVERSE-MERMAID – the lesser-known and
lesser-loved type of mermaid who sports a
generous-sized fish head and long lady legs.
**DOILIES – dainty lace cloths for putting
things on. Like a beer mat made by a spider.

## TENNESSEE TOM

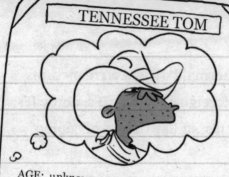

AGE: unknown

OCCUPATION: Cowboy and Man of Mystery

SPECIAL SKILLS: Horse shouting (similar to horse whispering but much louder).

HOBBIES: Wearing hats. Staring at the horizon.

CATCHPHRASE: 'Yup.'

## FELICITY FRUMP

AGE: ~~39~~ 39

OCCUPATION: Fairy Godmother

SPECIAL SKILLS: Can transform pumpkins into almost any other vegetable (so long as it's the same size and shape as a pumpkin).

HOBBIES: Bare-knuckle fight club.

CATCHPHRASES: 'Fiddlesticks!'
'Abra-kebabbage, that pumpkin is now a cabbage!'
'That's fightin' talk!'

There were articles on 'IF Accessories' and 'IF Grooming'. There was a letters page with questions from realsies around the world. There were recipes for 'IF Treats', tips on dental care and a big feature on the glitzy IFFY Awards. There was a news page from the C.L.I.F.F. Council*, who seemed to be the folks in charge. C.L.I.F.F. stood for the 'Corporate League of Imaginary Friends Federation', and they gave an update on the building work at their headquarters. (They'd recently installed elevators after several complaints that the firemen's poles were too difficult to climb.)

Martin couldn't put the catalogue down, fascinated by this whole new world. And several hours later he was still lying on his bed poring over its pages.

*C.L.I.F.F. COUNCIL – a group of mysterious individuals who rule over the imaginary world with an iron fist (or furry paw, or wet flipper, or flappy wing, or weird alien limb, or disgusting blob part, depending on the councillor).

It was at this point that he came to a full-page advertisement for *WhIF*'s 'IF of the Month'.

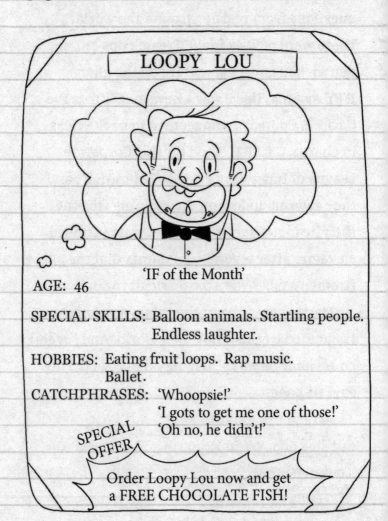

By the time Martin reached this page it was almost dinner time and he was feeling rather peckish. He stared at the special-offer flash at the bottom of the page. A free chocolate fish.

Martin had never eaten a chocolate fish.

He'd eaten a chocolate mouse, a chocolate frog, a chocolate hen, a chocolate bunny, even a chocolate bell. But never a chocolate fish.

He wondered what it would taste like.

Probably just like normal chocolate – but extra salty!

Martin stared at Loopy Lou and studied his smiling face.

Seems like a fun guy, he thought to himself. Looks friendly.

His eyes moved back to the special offer.

And I do *really* want that chocolate fish.

After a few moments he gave a final, decisive nod. Yes, this was the one. We had a winner.

'Loopy Lou and the chocolate fish will be my imaginary friend!' he declared triumphantly. He then grabbed a biro and carefully drew a big circle several times around the advertisement. Martin smiled at his handiwork, looking very satisfied with his choice.

Things were really happening now. He was finally getting himself a new pal. It wouldn't be just him against the world any more. It would be him and Loopy Lou and a chocolate fish against the world!

Things were looking up.

That evening, after dinner, Martin took the catalogue and made his way out to the back garden. He grabbed a shovel from the back wall by his father's workshop and dug a sizeable dent in the ground, whistling happily as he worked. Then, as Laurel had instructed, he laid the catalogue in the hole and covered it up. Once the soil and sods of grass were back in place, he stood back, quite pleased with the end result – you'd never have known there was an imaginary catalogue buried down there at all!

Finally he called out, 'Cork is the best! Cork is the best! Cork is the best! Cork is the best! Cork is the best! Cork is the best! . . .'

After he'd been doing this for a while, his father opened the door of his workshop and looked out.

'Martin?'

'Just a second, Dad,' said Martin, trying not to lose count. 'Cork is the best! Cork is the best! Cork is the best! Cork is the best! Cork is the best! Cork is the best! . . .'

Liam came out of the workshop and watched his son shouting at the ground. He was beginning to look quite concerned.

'Cork is the best! Cork is the best! Cork is the best! Cork is the best! Cork is the best!'

'Everything OK, pal?'

Martin paused and looked at his dad blankly. 'Yeah. Why?'

'Have you ever actually . . . been to Cork?'

'To be honest, Dad, I'm not even sure it's a real place. But I just need to shout it out twenty times.'

Liam frowned, trying not to look too worried. 'Right. Er . . . Are you missing school a lot, pal?' he asked gently.

'No, not really.'

'Ah yeah, we're all missing school,' Liam nodded, not listening. 'All this free time can make you kids get a bit . . . er . . .' He searched for words other than 'crazy', 'bananas', 'freaky', and then finally said, 'restless.'

'Well, rest easy, Dad,' said Martin brightly. 'Because something tells me that my life's about to get a whole lot better!'

Liam nodded and smiled, though he had no idea what his son was on about. 'OK, well, that's good.'

Martin headed back to the house and Liam returned to his workshop, not quite sure what to think.

A few moments later, Martin hurried back

to the hole, counting on his fingers, not quite finished. 'Cork is the best! Cork is the best! Cork is the best!'

He sprinted away just as the workshop door opened and Liam peered out, looking worried again.

# CHAPTER NINE
## LOOPY LOU

Martin woke up the next morning and was greeted by the most horrific sight he'd ever seen – his sister Sinead, semi-clothed, midway through getting dressed.

'Argh! My eyes!' he cried, and dived back underneath the duvet.

'Ya peeping pest!' she barked, and threw something at his head.

It was probably a shoe, but Martin decided not to investigate, preferring to remain in the darkness until she was gone. As he lay there, struggling to get the image of Sinead's back acne out of his brain, he forced himself to think about happy things instead – like the impending arrival of his imaginary friend.

'How will he arrive?' he wondered, trying

not to wonder about his sister's weird mole and tufts of shoulder hair. 'Will he just show up at the door? Or shimmy down the chimney? Or will he burrow into my brain like some kind of perky parasite?'

Just then Martin received a goodbye-dig-in-the-leg from Sinead.

'Ow!'

She chuckled to herself and plodded off down the hallway.

Martin threw aside the duvet and sat up, clutching his thigh. Even without seeing him, Sinead knew where to strike. She was a skilled dead-legger – he had to give her that.

Martin opened his wardrobe to get dressed. But instead of seeing his well-organized shirt and pants collection, he suddenly came face-to-face with a forty-six-year-old balding man in a purple coat and polka-dot* trousers, who beamed at him excitedly.

*POLKA-DOT – a pattern with loads and loads of dots. It's pronounced 'poke-a-dot'. The **L** is just there to confuse us, as if all those dots weren't confusing enough already.

'Loopy Lou in da house!!' he cried with joy, and leaped into Martin's arms.

'Arggh!' Martin screamed, and fell backwards on to the floor with the man on top of him.

'Whoopsie!' sang the man.

Martin gaped at him and tried to catch his breath, his little heart pounding in his chest. 'Lou?'

'*Loopy* Lou!' the IF yelled. 'Loopy like a fruity loop!'

He hopped to his feet and then launched into a kind of rap, dancing in a pair of big red shoes as he shouted the lyrics.

> *How do you do?*
> *I'm Loopy Lou!*
> What!?
> *Your brand-new*
> *Imaginary crew!*
> What!?
> *I said I'm Lou!*
> *I'm here for you!*
> Who?
> *Martin Moo!*
> *Cock-a-doodle-doo!*

He then stood there, grinning inanely, as if expecting some kind of applause. Martin lay on the ground, rather taken aback by Lou's big entrance.

'It's Moone,' said Martin. 'Not Moo.'

'Dammit!' shouted Lou. 'I didn't think you'd notice that. I should have gone with the other alternative: *I play kazoo!*'

He pulled out a kazoo and blew into it, making a long, loud honking noise. He then beamed at Martin enthusiastically, apparently waiting for a response.

Martin smiled back politely, though in truth he wasn't a big fan of kazoos. 'Well, it's nice to meet you, Lou,' he said, getting up from the floor and dusting off his pyjamas. He was pretty stunned that an imaginary friend had actually shown up, but he also couldn't help but notice that something was missing.

'So . . . do you have my free gift?' he asked hopefully.

'Your what's that now?'

'My chocolate fish.'

'Of course!' squealed Lou excitedly. 'Loopy Lou nearly forgots!'

He reached deep into a pocket of his purple

coat and withdrew a large chocolate mackerel by the tail.

'Catcheroo, Marty Moo!' he yelled, and tossed it to Martin.

Martin caught the fish, but it suddenly started writhing in his hands. The flippin' thing was alive! It was squirming and throwing itself around like it had just been pulled out of a river.

Martin dropped it in shock, and the fish flailed on the floor, slapping and thrashing its big chocolatey tail.

'Whoopsie!' sang Lou with amusement.

'It's alive!' cried Martin.

'Of course it's alive!' said Lou. 'I ain't gonna stiff you with no dead fish.'

The fish had managed to thrash its way over to the doorway and with another leap it hurled itself into the hall.

'It's getting away!' cried Martin in a panic. 'Kill it! Kill it!'

'*Kill* it?'

'Kill it!'

The pair ran out to the hallway and watched the fish floundering on the carpet.

'How do I kills it?' asked a confused Lou.

'I don't know. Hit it on the head or something!'

Lou pulled out his kazoo and chucked it at the fish.

'No, ya big eejit!' Martin blurted. 'With a hammer or something.'

'I gots to get me one of those!' chirped Lou.

'What?'

'It's one of my catchphrases,' he explained. 'Actually I do have a hammer! Here ya go.'

He pulled out a large inflatable hammer from inside his purple coat and handed it to Martin.

'Ah for – This isn't going to kill it!'

'Trust me,' Lou assured him. 'That hammer can dos a lot of damage.'

Martin sighed with frustration, but then pursued the flailing fish with the inflatable hammer. As he did this, his sister Fidelma passed by in her dressing gown and watched with confusion as Martin tried to whack an imaginary fish with an imaginary hammer. She opened her mouth to ask something, but then decided against it, and walked off.

Martin did actually manage to batter the fish a couple of times, but the hammer just bounced off it, and the fish flopped away into the bathroom.

'Don't let it gets to the loo!' squealed Lou.

But it was too late. The chocolate mackerel launched itself into the air and landed with a smack on top of the cistern*. It then grinned at the hapless pair, knowing that its escape was all but complete.

'Better luck next time, Moone-face!' it sneered, and flushed the toilet with its tail.

'No!' cried Martin.

*CISTERN – sounds almost like 'sister', but it's actually part of a toilet. Yes, it's quite noisy and can be a bit stinky, but it's got absolutely nothing to do with sisters.

'Sayonara\*, boys!' waved the fish as it dived into the churning water.

Martin ran to the bowl and peered inside, but the fish was gone, leaving nothing but a faint chocolate swirl in the water.

'Oh no, he didn't!' sang Lou.

But Martin was looking a lot less chirpy.

\*SAYONARA – Japanese for goodbye. But English-speakers aren't as polite as the Japanese, so when we say, 'Sayonara', it usually means, 'So long, suckers!

'My chocolate fish!' he wailed. 'I never even got to taste him.'

'We could have some of the toilet water?' suggested Lou.

'I'm not drinking out of the toilet,' said Martin as Lou started splashing him with bowl juice. 'Quit it, ya weird wacko!' Martin snapped, but Lou continued smiling stupidly.

'So what'll we do next?' Lou asked eagerly. 'Want me to make a balloon dog? Or put a frog on my head? Or make a dog eat a balloon frog? And then put the dog on my head and see if it poops out the frog?'

Martin glared at him coldly. 'That was all your fault. I was promised a chocolate fish and now I'm covered in toilet soup!' He stood up from the bowl in a huff. 'You need to calm the flip down.'

He thrust the inflatable hammer at Lou and stormed off.

Lou stared after Martin, his smile fading. 'Whoopsie,' he murmured.

*

Later that day, Martin decided to take a stroll into town to get some fresh air and maybe some chocolate that he could melt into the shape of a fish. He was halfway there when Loopy Lou jumped out of a hedge.

'Boo!'

Martin paused, still a bit annoyed. 'Oh. Hi.'

He walked on, and Lou jogged beside him, bouncing along in his clown shoes.

'Where ya off to, Marty Moo?'

'Just heading into town. I was thinking of checking out the new season's back-to-school stationery on offer. See what my protractor* options are for sixth class**.'

*PROTRACTOR – a clear plastic semicircle used to measure angles. It's very handy for doodling, fidgeting and back-scratching and can also be used as an emergency spoon for a yogurt.

**SIXTH CLASS – the final year of primary school in Ireland. Sixth-classers are the grand-daddies of school, the wise old bullfrogs, who then start secondary school and find that they are mere tadpoles again.

'Protractors? I gots to get me one of those!'

Martin said nothing and continued walking.

The pair were silent for a few moments, and then Lou spoke in quite a normal voice. 'Listen, Martin, I think we got off on the wrong foots. I'm sorry about the fishy, I really am. All I want is to be the best imaginary friend ever. Is there any chance we can shake hands and start again?'

Martin stopped and looked at him. Lou offered his hand, and Martin couldn't help but feel a bit guilty.

'You're right, Lou,' he said. 'I'm sorry too.'

'Put it there, partner.' Lou smiled, and Martin shook his hand.

*BUZZZZZ!*

Martin whipped his hand away as Lou squealed with laughter, holding up his palm, which held a dodgy-looking hand-buzzer. 'Whoopsie! I done me some magics!' the IF sang, as he danced around with glee.

'That's not magic. It's just a flippin' hand-buzzer,' retorted Martin.

'Loopy Lou made it himself!' Lou beamed proudly. 'Want me to buzzy you again?'

Martin rolled his eyes and walked off.

Loopy Lou bounded after him. 'Hey, Moo-Moo! Wait for me!'

That day turned out to be one of the most exhausting days of Martin's life. As he browsed the aisles of BetterBuys*, Lou bounced around the shop like a tightly wound jack-in-the-box, constantly startling Martin by jumping around corners and leaping off shelves. Poor Martin couldn't remotely focus on his stationery needs, so wandered around town instead. But Lou followed him everywhere like an overexcited balding puppy, performing useless bits of 'magic', making up lame rap songs and offering Martin an endless supply of balloon animals.

*BETTERBUYS – a local shop that specializes in flogging anything from certain books to curtain hooks, woks to socks and nearly nothing in between.

When they finally returned home, Martin turned to Lou abruptly. 'Well, this is my place, Lou. See ya now!'

He hurried inside and shut the front door, leaving Lou standing outside with a confused expression. Martin stood in the hall and breathed a sigh of relief.

'Boo!' shouted Lou through the letter box.

Martin rubbed his forehead. He was getting a headache. He crouched down and spoke to Lou through the door. 'Look, how long does this go on for?'

'What do you mean, Moo-Moo?'

'What time do you quit for the day?'

'Quit?! Loopy Lou *never* quits!'

Martin's shoulders sagged. 'Oh balls,' he murmured, and moved off into the kitchen.

His mother was looking in the fridge and glanced over at him.

'Hey, love. What do you fancy for dinner tonight?'

'I dunno,' he mumbled, and slumped down at the kitchen table.

'Come on,' she said. 'I'll make us something nice for the craic. You can have *anything* you want, just name it . . .'

Martin frowned, trying to imagine what he'd like. But his imagination was utterly exhausted. He could see Lou outside the kitchen window trying to put on a puppet show with two balloon animals.

'I dunno,' said Martin again, trying to remember the names of any types of food. 'Bread?'

'Bread?' asked Debra, a little surprised. 'O-kaaay. And what would you like with that?'

Martin racked his depleted brain again, wincing like he was in pain. 'Water?'

'Bread and water?'

Martin nodded. 'That sounds lovely, Mam.'

'Hey, Moo-meister! Look at me!' shouted Lou through the window, pretending he was walking down a set of steps as he disappeared under the window ledge. But Martin just laid his head on the kitchen table and closed his eyes.

'My head's a pineapple!' yelled Loopy Lou.

Martin did his best to ignore him. But he knew this couldn't go on. He'd made a terrible mistake, and he had no one to blame but himself.

Then, as he thought about it more, he realized there *was* someone else he could blame – Padraic! It was Padraic who had started all of this, and so it was Padraic who should flippin' well fix it.

## CHAPTER TEN
## PLAN B

The next day Martin found the road to Padraic's house to be particularly messy. There were rubbish bags filled with cans of beans, empty tins of Spam and peas, and eggshells covered in rotten smells. It reminded him that it was the day before the bin men came. Which reminded him that it was a Thursday. Which meant that it had now been FIVE WHOLE DAYS since he'd started this ridiculous IF-escapade and he was now even worse off than when he began.

It's a disgrace! he thought to himself. This is all Padraic's fault. What kind of an idiot can't sort me out with a decent imaginary friend?' Martin rounded the corner, and saw exactly what kind of an idiot he was dealing with.

Padraic had a big mop of hair, very much

like a mop. Most days it fell lazily down to about his ear lobes, but on this particular day it rose sharply to about half a foot above his forehead. Padraic's gruaige* was highly on end.

'Oh howya, Martin, good timing. I'm nearly finished checking the electric fence for faults.'

'What do ya mean?' asked a concerned Martin.

'Well, each week, I have to go around the perimeter of the farm and touch every fence to make sure that it's shocking properly.'

'Right . . . But isn't that a little bit dangerous, P?'

'A little bit?! Haha . . . A *little* bit?!!

*GRUAIGE – Pronounced 'grew-a-gah'. The Irish word for hair. In Ireland, many people have red hair. This is of course because the first-ever Irish woman married a fire extinguisher.

HAHAHAHAHAHAHAHAHAHA!'

It was a terribly long and loud laugh, which kinda worried Martin.

'You laughed quite loud for a while there, Padraic.'

'Yeah,' he chirped. 'I suppose I did, hahaha.'

Padraic began walking to the next electric fence on his route, skipping past Martin and giggling like a giddy giraffe.

Martin was concerned for his friend, but he was even more concerned about his own useless imaginary friend, so he decided to get right to the business at hand.

'Listen, P, I'm having some troubles with my IF.'

'Really?' asked Padraic. 'Are his headlocks too tight? Been there, pal, been there.'

Before Martin could correct him, Padraic walked off, throwing a twitchy half star-jump into his stride every now and again as he went.

'The best thing to do is to have a release word,' Padraic continued. 'Whenever your

IF hears you use that word, they have to free you from their cranium crush. Now, the key to a good release word is . . . complexity. You need to make it as different from the normal words you use as possible. The phrase we're using at the moment is "frangipani sandwich".' Padraic ambled on, blathering away. '"What's a frangipani sandwich?" I hear you ask. Well, Martin, I have no idea, and I don't care because the sandwich is irrelevant – so stop asking stupid questions. All that matters is that Crunchie lets go whenever I shout it. Before that it was "tarantula lipstick". I like to change it twice a week, to keep him on his toes. The only problem is, I often forget to tell Crunchie. So he just presumes I'm muttering nonsense while I'm trying not to faint. But sure it's all just a bit of craic.'

Padraic turned to face his pal and only then realized that Martin was still standing where he left him, twenty paces back.

'Did you catch any of that?' he asked.

'Something about a sandwich?' Martin offered.

'Close enough. God but it's a lovely starry day today, isn't it?'

'You mean you're seeing stars?' asked Martin, catching up with him.

'Aren't you? Look, there's Orion. And Ursa Major.' He pointed up at the bright, grey, starless morning sky. 'And over there . . . I think the moon just winked at me.'

'Yeaaah . . .' replied a worried Martin. 'Listen, P, this new IF of mine, Loopy Lou, is a loony tune. He's driving me nuts.'

'What's wrong with him?'

'He's too flippin' wacky. And needy. He needs a good whack!'

'Oh no. Is he the kind of fella who calls himself "mad"?'

'He's exactly that kind of fella!'

'Oh, I hate that sort. They're the worst people in the world.'

'Yeah. When I left the house this morning, he was licking the wallpaper to find out what flavour it was.'

'Well, it sounds like someone's got a case of realsie remorse*,' Padraic said as he reached the next electric fence.

'And that someone is me.' Martin nodded. 'But what can I do? I mean, I can try to house-train him, I suppose, but the bottom line is, I don't want a male companion whose life's ambition is to tickle a unicorn to death.'

Now, to be fair to Loopy Lou, what he'd actually said was, 'Boy, oh boy, I'd sure die happy if I could knock a crazy horn-horse down with my funny feather!!!' Which could have meant a few different things. But given that Lou was answering Martin's simple question, 'Did you see my other shoe anywhere, Lou?' the details don't really matter. Martin had adopted a lunatic**.

*REALSIE REMORSE – similar to 'Buyer's Remorse', except you don't get a receipt with a misspent imagination.
**LUNATIC – a crazy person. Originally referred to people who shouted at the moon or thought that the moon winked at them.

'Just get another one,' Padraic said plainly, as he squatted into electric-fence testing position.

'Wait . . . I can get another IF?!'

'Ah yeah, I think you're allowed one more go these days. They had to change the rules after a girl in Austria circled the page number in the IF catalogue and two numbers turned up in her wardrobe.'

As the word 'wardrobe' left his lips, Padraic tentatively placed his hand on the electric fence. Nothing happened. Shock-free. He happily made a note of it in his fence folder.

'Well, that changes everything!' said a delighted Martin. 'That's exactly what I'll do. I'll pick another IF. I'll dig up the catalogue, watch *Airwolf**, maybe have a bath, then get on with the task of making the most important choice of my young life. Again.'

*AIRWOLF – a popular TV show from the 1980s where a wolf flew a helicopter. The follow-up show, *Sea Donkey*, proved less popular.

Martin turned to head home, determined
and excited about what lay ahead. But what lay
directly ahead right now was the electric fence,
which he stupidly tried to hop over – but didn't
quite make it.

'AAAjjJkKkKRRGGhhhxxxxAAf%%hdbw,' he
shrieked.

He writhed around for quite a while, like a
raisin in a current. 'AhahhshshaknohbaLLS!'

'I see you're caught up in the electric fence
there, Martin.'

'VVVereiudbsmn,££%$&sffdededdh!' Martin yelped.

'C'mon fence, let him go, he's only a boy,' Padraic barked at the horizontal electric wire.

'LLLxaxaxaxyHELP^$2nbn!' muttered the horizontal electric squire.

'Fence! Don't make me ask you again!' ordered Padraic.

As Martin's hair pinged out like fingers from a hairy glove, Padraic approached, stopped and whispered, 'Frangipani sandwich, fence.'

## CHAPTER ELEVEN
## A NEW IF

Martin returned home on his fart-cycle to find Loopy Lou sitting in the front garden. He was peering up at the sky, sketching in a copybook, looking quite perplexed. Crumpled balls of paper lay all around him.

'Dammit, Lou!' he berated himself, and then furiously rubbed out part of his drawing.

Martin ditched his bike in the shrubbery and headed over. 'Hi, Lou, how are you getting on?' he asked. 'Did you get all those clouds drawn?'

Lou jumped, looking a bit panicked, as if he hadn't expected the boss to be back quite so soon. 'Oh. Er. Well, actually I'm still working on the first one. The damn things keep changing shape, Marty Moo!' he wailed, and held up his work-in-progress.

Martin looked up at the summer sky, where a few fluffy, cumulus clouds* were drifting lazily overhead, like a herd of fluffy, lazy sheep.

'I'm trying to draw the one that looks like a cake,' explained Loopy Lou.

'You mean that one that looks like a shoe?'

*CUMULUS CLOUDS – soft, bouncy clouds that often look like other things. This means they are filled with wonder and possibility. These are a rare sight in Ireland, which specializes in stratus clouds, which are filled with drizzle and disappointment.

Lou looked up at the sky. 'Arrghhh!' he yelled in frustration, ripping out the page and crumpling it up.

Martin couldn't help but feel a little guilty. He'd needed to distract Lou so he could escape to Padraic's house, but he hadn't expected his IF to devote himself so fully to the task.

'Well, you can give up now if you want, Lou,' Martin told him kindly.

'No! I know this is important to you, Moo-Moo. Or you wouldn't have asked me to do it.'

'Er . . . That's right.'

'I'll get it done, don't you worry. Loopy Lou never quits!'

Martin felt bad. But he was also very keen to head into the back garden, dig up the catalogue, and order himself a

replacement for this cloud-drawing klutz – a plan that so filled him with excitement that it was giving him itchy shovel-fingers*. So he just shrugged happily. 'Okey-dokey. Keep up the good work!' And ran off towards the house.

Loopy Lou looked back at the sky and sighed wearily when he saw that the shoe-cloud had now turned back into a cake.

A little later, Martin was in the back garden, digging up the catalogue. Or at least he was trying to. But he'd forgotten where he'd buried it, so he was now covered in muck and was digging his seventeenth hole.

Liam was observing him from the kitchen window as he waited for the kettle to boil.

'What's Martin doing out there?' he asked, with a little concern in his voice.

Debra was at the kitchen table, but didn't

*ITCHY SHOVEL-FINGERS – a term for someone's eagerness to dig a hole. This should not be confused with 'itchy hole-digging-fingers' which is a term for someone who keeps pulling their underwear out of their bum.

bother looking up from her *Roscommon Herald*\*. 'Some form of kung fu?' she guessed. 'Body-boarding?'

'He's digging up the garden.'

Debra gave a sigh and joined Liam at the window. 'Ah, he's probably just lost a bone or something,' she said.

The kettle boiled and she began to make a pot of tea. Liam continued to watch Martin with a disappointed frown. There was a time when he'd had high hopes for his only son. But he'd long since put those dreams to bed. And then smothered them sadly with a pillow.

'You don't think he's going a bit mad, do you?' he asked.

Debra glanced at him. 'What, like properly mad? Or just summer-time mad\*\*?'

'Well, he's definitely summer-time mad.'

---

\***ROSCOMMON HERALD** – fancy fish 'n' chip paper handed out weekly in ironed form.

\*\***SUMMER-TIME MAD** – a type of craziness that sets in when children have too much freedom. Symptoms include whistling, daydreaming, kite-making, raft-building, excessive laughter and too much general happiness.

'Ah yeah, he's been summer-time mad since about mid-July.'

'Damn school holidays,' said Liam, shaking his head. 'They just never end.'

Debra nodded grimly in agreement. 'I mean, a week is nice. Ten days even. But two months off school is just—'

'Barbaric,' said Liam. 'Barbaric is what it is. I mean, look at him. Digging away like some kind of demented mole.' Just then, Martin stood up and gave a yowl of delight, not unlike a demented mole. He ran in through the back door, gripping the catalogue triumphantly.

'I found it! I found it!' he cried.

His parents looked at his empty hand, waving the imaginary catalogue in the air.

'Found what?' asked Debra.

Martin paused, suddenly realizing that he'd let his excitement get the better of him. He swiftly tucked the catalogue behind his back.

'Er . . . nothing,' he replied, not suspiciously at all.

He stood there for another moment, and then ran out.

Liam shook his head. 'See what I mean?' he said. 'No work and all play makes Jack go flippin' bananas.'

That evening Martin lay on his bed and pored over the catalogue once again. This time he was an educated buyer. A discerning customer. This time he knew what he wanted. And it was about as far away from Loopy Lou as he could get. What he needed was someone more low-key. Laid-back. Less bouncy and colourful. Basically, a less imaginative imaginary friend.

Just then there was a friendly knock from the inside of the wardrobe – a rather musical *rat-a-tat-tat-tat-tat*!

To most people this would have been a little freaky. But Martin was getting used to a certain amount of traffic moving through his wardrobe, so didn't think much of it. He hopped to his feet and opened the door to find a tall man stooped inside it, wearing a cheap suit and holding a clipboard. He was a strikingly handsome fella with piercing blue eyes, a nicely toned beard, a jaunty red woolly hat and a manly, jowly face. That's right – it was me!

'Hello there. I'm Customer Service Representative 263749. But you can call me CustServRep263 for short,' I said to Martin, and glanced at my clipboard, 'You must be Melvin Goone.'

'Melvin Goone?' asked the little fella. 'Er, no, I'm Martin Moone. You must have the wrong wardrobe.'

'Moone?' I frowned suspiciously – it sounded like a made-up name to me. But I dug in my jacket pocket, and, sure enough, there was another clipboard with his name on it. 'Ah! Here we go. Martin Paul Kenny Dalglish Moone?' I asked, looking over his details.

'That's me,' answered the boy. 'Although most people just call me . . . Eagle . . . Power . . . Face.'

'Do people really call you that?' I queried.

'Sure they do. I have loads of cool nicknames at school,' Martin replied tentatively.

'Such as . . . ?'

'Oh . . . er . . . Lion Man. The Mirthanator. Peach Spit.'

'Peach Spit?' I asked, getting the feeling this was the only true one.

'Yeah, I spilled a peach yogurt on myself when I was in third class,' Martin explained, embarrassed.

To save the child from further memory-induced embarrassment I decided to move on from the nickname convo* and continue with the paperwork.

'So, Martin Moone, am I right in saying you dug up your catalogue?'

'You are indeed.' He nodded.

*CONVO – short for conversation. But the fact that I need to explain it really means that convo is *long* for conversation.

I ticked a box in my report. 'Lovely stuff. I'm here from Customer Service,' I explained. 'Mind if I come in? Your wardrobe's a little cramped and it smells like a fart's fungus in here.'

'Ah yes, that'd be Sinead's Girl Guide boots – she likes to let them air out in there. Come on in, beard-face!'

He stood back and I hopped into his bedroom.

# CHAPTER TWELVE
## CUSTOMER SERVICE
### REPRESENTATIVE 263749

Martin's brow was furrowed with confusion.

'So . . . you're saying, whenever a realsie digs up their catalogue, Customer Service sends someone to check up on them?'

'Yep,' I nodded. 'Standard procedure. Basically, digging up your catalogue is kind of like ringing an alarm bell.'

'In what way?'

'Well, it rings an alarm bell,' I explained. 'In my work cubicle. Which is pretty annoying.'

'Right.'

'So let's get on with this questionnaire,' I said, holding up my clipboard. 'What was the reason for digging up your catalogue? Was it:

A. Accidental.

B. Because you're thinking of exchanging your IF.

C. Just cos you wanted to read it again.

D. General stupidity.'

He was a dopey-looking kid, so my pencil was already hovering over D.

'B,' said Martin.

I peered at him, surprised. 'You were very quick to answer there. Are ya sure it wasn't D?'

'No, definitely B.'

'I'll tell ya what – I'll put a tick beside both of them, just to be sure.' I ticked B and D, and moved on. 'Next question – how satisfied are you with your imaginary friend? Are you:

A. Extremely satisfied.

B. Fairly satisfied.

C. Really quite unhappy.

D. Crying yourself to sleep.'

'I'm not one bit satisfied!' complained Martin. 'Loopy Lou is the worst imaginary friend ever! He's annoying, and loud, and stupid, and he smells weird, and he never shuts up, and his jokes are awful, and his magic is terrible, and if he makes another balloon animal I think I'm going to have to kick him!'

'So . . . B?' I asked tentatively.

'And worst of all, I never even got to eat the chocolate fish!'

'OK, I can't help you with the chocolate fish. Special promotions are a whole different department.'

'Look, I just want to exchange him!' declared Martin bluntly. 'I want a new IF!'

'Right. Understood.' I nodded. 'So B . . . with a little bit of C?'

Just then we heard Loopy Lou bounding down the hallway. 'Loopy Lou in da house!'

'Oh balls!' whispered Martin, looking flustered. Unsure what to do, he grabbed my clipboard and chucked it behind the bed.

'All finished!' hollered Lou, as he flounced through the door and thrust his latest cloud picture into Martin's hands.

'Oh. Er. Lovely stuff.' Martin nodded, barely glancing at the drawing.

Lou then noticed me standing there.

''Allo, 'allo, 'allo,' he said in a silly Cockney* voice. I could already see why Martin was having problems with this guy.

I smiled politely back at him.

He turned to Martin. 'Who's this big galloo?'

Martin's face reddened, unsure how to explain. 'He's, er . . .'

I shuffled my feet uncomfortably. 'Well, this is awkward.'

*COCKNEY - a traditional London dialect. It gets its name because the accent sounds like a cockerel being kneed in the head by a hen.

'He's, er . . .' Martin continued, but was clearly not the greatest of liars.

I decided to help him out. 'I'm, er, just here on business from—'

'Customer Service!' Martin blurted out, accidentally telling the truth.

Lou looked at me, a little concerned now. 'Customer Service? Loopy Lou isn't in trouble, I hopes?'

'No, no,' I assured him. 'I'm just, er, checking to see . . . how customers are appreciating the new . . . font. In the catalogue.'

'That's right! We're doing a font questionnaire!' nodded Martin.

'Oh,' said Lou. 'Where is it?'

'I threw it behind the bed,' explained Martin. *Idiot.*

'Want me to fetch it for you, Moo-Moo?'

'No, that's OK.'

'Do you know what'd be great, Lou?' I said, stepping in. 'All this font talk is making us pretty thirsty. Any chance you could head out and get us . . . a nice glass of, er . . .'

'Milk!' shouted Martin unhelpfully.

I went on. 'Or something more difficult to get, like . . .'

'Water!' suggested Martin, then realized his mistake. 'Er, no. Wait – not water, not from here. Water from miles away! From the sea!'

'Sea . . . water?' I asked.

'That's the one!' he nodded. 'I'd love a nice big glass of seawater,' he told Lou.

Lou seemed a bit thrown. 'But that's . . . kinda far, Marty Moo, and I don't have my honky-tonk horse.'

'Nah, it's not too far, Lou,' I lied. 'And the sooner you leave, the sooner you'll be back!'

'Well, I want to be back right now, so I better get outta here!' he cried with some urgency. He hurried out of the room, then turned and popped his big stupid head back around the door, 'Hey, Marty!' he squeaked. 'Ya want me to wrangle some tasty starfish too?'

'Starfish?' asked Martin.

'Yeah, Marty. Nothin' tastier than a couple of bony starfish sandwiches with wasp honey! I love those yummy dummies!'

'Actually, I'm good, Lou, thanks.'

'Suit yourself, ya big booboo! I gotta gets me one of those!' Lou left with a fart and skipped away.

Martin looked relieved. 'That was some excellent lying, CustServRep263.'

'Thank you! Wish I could say the same for you.'

I went to retrieve the questionnaire and came back to find Martin looking at the catalogue. He stared at it for a moment, thinking, and then turned to me. 'You know what? I've just had another one of my brilliant ideas.'

That seemed unlikely, but I said nothing.

'Forget all these crazy nut jobs. I think *you* should be my imaginary friend!' he announced.

'Me?!'

'Well, you're imaginary, aren't you? And you

seem a lot less annoying than Loopy Lou.'

'Well, yes, I'm imaginary, but I'm not an "imaginary friend". I do paperwork and stuff, I'm more of an imaginary clerk.'

'Not any more you're not! You work for me now!' cried Martin, and threw my questionnaire behind the bed again.

'Do you have to keep doing that? It's my favourite clipboard.'

'Come on, CustServRep263,' urged Martin. 'Help me out. I'm overrun with women in this house and I'm in dire need of a decent wingman before school starts up again. I've only got one more chance with this IF thing, and I don't want to risk another Lou situation. I want you on Team Martin. So, what do you say? Want to be my IF?'

I paused for a moment, thinking it over.

To be honest, I'd always wanted to be an imaginary friend. But this wasn't quite how I'd imagined it. Did I really want to be an IF to this little dope? I'd always imagined my realsie being someone who really needed me – like some poor kid in Africa. How else was I going to win an IFFY* award for being Best IF? Winning an IFFY is a tricky business. They don't just give them out to anyone, no sir.

So I decided to ask Martin a few more questions to see how he fitted into my IFFY plan.

'Are we in Africa right now?'

'Not right now, no.'

'Are we likely to move to Africa?'

'Probably not.'

'Would you say you're living in poverty?'

'No, I'd say I'm living in Boyle.'

'Do you have any incurable diseases?'

'No, I think all my diseases are curable. Except for maybe my foot warts.'

'Have you ever had a near-death experience?'

'I ate my lunch in a graveyard once?'

*IFFY – the annual back-slapping procession for imaginary friends. Similar to the Oscars in almost no way at all.

I'm not going to lie, I was a little underwhelmed by the Moone boy. He really didn't strike me as IFFY material. On the other hand, maybe this could be a kind of stepping stone to get me out of Customer Service . . .

I mulled it over a bit more, and then finally gave him a smile.

'All right, Martin – actually . . . are you totally committed to the name Martin?'

'Well, it's written on most of my underpants,' replied the child, worried.

'OK . . . well, what the heck?! Let's do this!'

Martin smiled happily. 'That's the best news I've heard today! Wait, what day is today?'

'Friday?' I offered.

'That's the best news I've heard *this week*!' he proclaimed, happier than I'd seen him since I got here. He shook my hand warmly. 'Welcome to my imagination!'

# CHAPTER THIRTEEN
## LAST DAYS OF SUMMER

The next morning, I was curled up on the floor at the foot of Martin's bed when my watch-alarm started beeping. I hopped to my feet, ready to begin my first day as an imaginary friend. But I soon discovered that Martin was not exactly an early riser. I admired this greatly, and went back to sleep, smiling at the thought of all those imaginary clerks trudging into the huge grey Customer Service tower block and squeezing into their miserable little cubicles. I could just imagine my boss, Mr Scabnose, glaring at my empty desk furiously. 'CustServRep263!! Where the gooples is CustServRep263?!' he'd demand. And all the other imaginary clerks would just shrug blankly. 'I dunno, Mr Scabnose, sir. At lunch?'

Hahaha! Oh, I was at lunch all right – the longest, laziest lunch of my life! It was such a treat to hop off the hamster-wheel of life and just kick back with this dozy little dormouse instead.

'I've noticed that you enjoy a generous sleep, Martin,' I told him, when he finally awoke from his slumber. 'You're a bit of a snooze glutton. A nap addict.'

'Oh, you're not wrong there,' he agreed. 'If I don't get a solid fourteen hours every night, I start to get the shakes. Sleep is my craic. It's the best craic ever!'

CUSTOMER SERVICE
REPRESENTATIVE : 263749

Over the next few days I learned about every detail of Martin's life – about his little town in the middle of nowhere, his trio of psychotic sisters and even his simple hopes and dreams – like owning a factory of space monkeys or inventing the first edible car.

I was also informed of his full list of allergies, which took up most of a morning.

'X-rays,' he declared, finally approaching the end. 'Yachts. Yaks. Yams. Zinc,' he went on. 'Zits. Zest* of lemons. Zest of limes. Zest in general. Zombies. And certain types of zoos. Mainly ones with yaks in them.'

'How do you know you're allergic to zombies?' I asked.

'Well I get a bit fluey every time I touch old people, and they're pretty similar, so I'm making an educated guess there, CustServRep263.'

*ZEST – the outer part of a fruit that's scraped off to flavour food. The human equivalent would probably be scabs, which can also add some zing to a dull dinner.

'Right.'

'Hey, shouldn't you be writing this stuff down?'

'Oh, I am,' I assured him.

He looked at me, noting that I was taking no notes.

'Mentally,' I added, tapping my forehead. 'In my Mental Notepad.'

'Ah, yes,' he nodded, impressed. 'Been meaning to get one of those. For when I've used up my Skin Notepad.'

He held up his hand and then scrawled on it: 'Get Mental Notepad.'

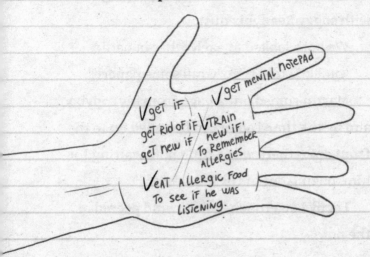

Life was pretty good, and we were really enjoying the last few days of Martin's summer holidays, but there was one dark cloud on the horizon. Actually there were a lot of dark clouds – this country seemed to specialize in miserable weather – but this cloud was more of a loud, annoying, polka-dot sort. And it blustered up the Moone driveway one day, just as Martin was tucking into his mid-afternoon bowl of Readybix.

'Yoohoo! Marty Moo! You home?' called Loopy Lou as he skipped towards the house trying not to spill his glass of seawater.

'He's back!' blurted Martin, spraying me with soggy Readybix dust.

We both looked at each other in panic.

'Quick!' I told him. 'Grab some paper!'

Martin ripped out a page from his copybook, and by the time Loopy Lou bounded up to the front door, there was a little note waiting for him, poking out of the letter box.

Loopy Lou crouched down and peered at the note.

'He's gone whale walking?' exclaimed Lou excitedly. 'The lucky ducky! I loves strolling around on their big stupid heads! I wonder if he'll be back soon,' he pondered. 'Maybe I should wait here.'

I'm not here.

I've gone for a walk.

~~Down the Road.~~

In Wales.

He was mulling this over when he noticed another note poking out of the letter box and bent down to read it.

'Oh. Well, I bet he'll be thirsty after all that whale walking. I wonders . . . Should I wait for him here anyway? Or should I wait at the sea? Hmmm. Here or at the sea . . . ?'

No, don't wait here, I won't be back for ages.

He then noticed yet another note that he hadn't noticed before. It read:

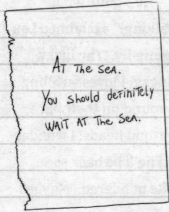

AT THE SEA.
You should definitely
WAIT AT THE SEA.

'Well, I guess it's back to the sea for me!' he beamed. 'What a helpful set of notes. Thanks, Mr Letter Box!'

He bounded away, and we peered through the letter box, watching him go.

'Why is he still here?' asked a worried Martin.

I shook my head. 'I don't get it. Usually when a realsie picks a new IF, the old one just vanishes.'

'So why didn't that happen?'

'I don't know.' I shrugged honestly.

'But you're in Customer Service! Shouldn't you know this stuff?'

'To be honest, Martin, I was never exactly . . . *superb* at my job. All that technical stuff is in the Big Massive Manual, which I always meant to read, but never actually did.'

'Why not?

'Cos it's full of useless information that no one ever needs! Apart from right now,' I admitted. 'Look, why don't you just tell him? Tell him he's not your IF any more.'

'Are you crazy?'

'Am *I* crazy?!' asked Martin's mother.

She was standing in the hallway, looking down at her son, who was kneeling on the floor, peering out through the letter box with a worried expression.

'Oh. Er. Hi, Mam,' Martin said with a wave, hopping to his feet. 'No, I was just talking to the letter box. What you got there?' he asked, looking at a stack of books in her arms.

'Got all your new books for school.'

'Aw, thanks, Mam!' He smiled, taking them from her. 'I love the smell of new books.' He breathed in deeply, but then started coughing violently. 'Ugh. What is that stench?'

She looked a bit guilty. 'Er, well, when I say "new" books, I mean they're new . . . to you.'

'Oh, for – Are these hand-me-down* books?' cried Martin.

'I spat in four of them!' shouted Sinead from the kitchen.

Trisha called over from the television. 'I think I wrote a few good poems about Satan in that maths book, Martin.'

Fidelma yelled from somewhere else. 'Oh, and I might have Tipp-Exed out all the dates in that history book – to test myself.'

'Oh balls,' moaned Martin in despair. 'I should've known . . .'

'Ah, love,' said Debra sadly, 'you know we can't afford to buy new books. It's hard enough that you're a boy and won't wear their old knickers.'

'Yeah, ya selfish fancy-pants!' shouted Trisha.

*HAND-ME-DOWN – second-hand. If you're posh. If you're not, there's a fair chance that several more hands and a few smelly feet have also been involved.

'But, Mam, I'm starting sixth class now,' pleaded Martin. 'This is the big league. I need proper pants *and* proper books. Ones that haven't been gnawed on by Sinead.'

'Ah, Martin, the books are grand. Just stick a bit of wallpaper* around them. That'll spruce them up nicely.'

She popped a large roll of old wallpaper on top of his pile and the two of us trudged out of the room with the stack of sister-soiled books.

'They smell like Death's farts,' I told him. (And I knew that for a fact. We were once stuck in a lift together.)

*WALLPAPER - school books are often wallpapered in Ireland to protect them from harm. When placed beside walls, the books are therefore camouflaged, so can never be found, and thus never be damaged.

Martin spent much of his last free weekend trying to decontaminate his new books. Between them, the Moone girls had befouled almost every page. He spent hours rubbing out Fidelma's answers, Tipp-Exing over Trisha's satanic scrawls and scraping off Sinead's food remains. It seemed that she'd been particularly peckish that year, as several books had been chewed at the edges and many pages were missing their corners.

It wasn't exactly how we'd planned to spend the last weekend of his summer holidays, but things were about to get even worse. Just as he was covering his geography book in flowery wallpaper, we heard a familiar voice outside.

'Moo-Moo! You're back!'

Martin jumped, and turned to see Loopy Lou's barmy, beaming face peering through the window.

'Oh. Hi, Lou!'

Lou's smile faded when he saw that Martin was not alone. 'Why's the Customer Service dum-dum still here, Marty? You still talking about fonts?'

Martin and I looked at each other. 'Er. He was just . . . leaving,' said Martin.

'Great! I'm coming in, Marty!' cried Lou, and bounded away towards the back door.

'We've got to get rid of him,' said Martin.

I shook my head wearily. 'So what's the plan here? Just keep sending him back to the sea forever?'

'Maybe.'

'You've got to fire him, buddy. Maybe then he'll disappear.'

'But I don't think he'll like that.'

'No, he probably won't,' I agreed. 'But you're a man now, Martin. You're in sixth class. And if you're going to run a space-monkey factory some day, then you've got to get used to firing people.'

Martin looked very nervous at this thought. He might have done battle every day with his sisters, but he wasn't actually fond of confrontation, and the notion of firing Lou made him squirm with unease.

'Look, just take him out for lunch or something. Somewhere nice, so he won't make a scene. And just tell him how it is.'

'But what if he goes bananas?'

'He's a professional, right? I'm sure he'll handle it just fine.'

Just then, Lou cartwheeled into the room.

'Marty, I got ya your yummy seawater, but

then a crazy horn-horse bumped me in the
bottom and I spilled it all over my belly
buttons!'

'Hi, Lou.' Martin smiled nervously. 'Want
to . . . go to lunch?'

# CHAPTER FOURTEEN
# THE BREAK-UP

'Well, this is an unexpected treaty treat!' Lou beamed happily. 'Pretty fanceroo!'

'Er, yeah,' nodded Martin, with a glance around. 'It's not too shabby all right.'

They were sitting in the middle of the Boyle Bistro, which was completely deserted. It was a small, greasy sort of place, the kind that specialized in fried breakfasts, but Loopy Lou was gazing around in awe, clearly pleased with their surroundings. He'd even decided to wear a small bowler hat* for the occasion.

'You know, not many IFs get taken out to fancy-pants restaurants by their realsie.

*BOWLER HAT – the official head-wear for all ten-pin bowlers. This is because if your bowling ball ever gets stuck in the machine, you can simply bowl your hat instead.

152

I must have really impressed you!'

Martin gave a nervous chuckle. 'Haha. Yeah.' He glanced around again. 'Although, I think it's more of a "cafe".'

'Ooh. A *café, madame*,' said Lou, even more impressed. He put on a posh voice and clicked his fingers, pretending to order. 'Five lobster milkshakes, please!'

Martin laughed at this, but stopped abruptly when he noticed the waitress standing right beside him.

'Oh. Hi there,' he said, a bit startled.

She was looking at him with a confused expression, holding a pad and pencil.

'Ready to order?' she asked.

'We are indeed,' replied Martin, picking up the menu.

'We?'

He looked back at her, thrown for a moment. 'I mean – I. *I* am indeed. And *you* are ready to take my order. So *we* are both ready. Was what I meant.'

She frowned slightly, but let it go.

'Nice save, Moo-Moo,' grinned Loopy Lou, and then added in a posh voice, 'I doff my hat to thee.'

He doffed his hat, raising it slightly, and a frog slid off his head on to the table.

'Whoopsie!' he sang. 'I done me some frog magic!'

Martin looked up at the waitress, who was still waiting to take his order. She could see neither Lou nor the frog that was hopping around the table, and Martin was doing his best to ignore both of them.

'Em. I'll have a red lemonade,' he told the waitress. 'And er . . .'

He looked at Lou questioningly.

'Ah yes,' said Lou, consulting the menu. 'I would like a bowl of a chimp chowder, served in a swan's armpit .'

Martin turned back to the waitress. 'And a Fanta.'

The waitress frowned. 'A red lemonade *and* a Fanta?'

'Yes, please.' Martin nodded.

'At the same time?'

'Er, yes. I'm really . . . parched.'

There was a pause as the waitress looked at Martin. It was clear that there was something odd about this little twerp, but at least his order was simple enough, so she just shrugged and wandered off to retrieve the drinks.

'Fanta's boring!' complained Loopy Lou, watching the frog leap off the table and hop away. 'Aren't we gonna have some fun, Marty Moo?'

'Actually, er,' said Martin nervously, 'I thought we should have a bit of a chat.'

'A chat? About whats?'

'About us.'

Loopy Lou frowned, and for the first time a worried look crossed his features. 'Whats about us?' he asked.

'Well, the thing is, Lou . . .' began Martin, fidgeting uneasily with his fork, 'it's just not working out.'

'What's not working out?'

'Us,' said Martin, looking down. 'Us is not working out.'

'What does that means?' asked Lou. 'That ain't even not a proper sentence!'

Martin looked at him apologetically. 'I'm going to have to let you go.'

Lou gaped at him, shell-shocked. He looked as if he'd been kicked in the stomach by one of his big stupid clown shoes. 'You're . . . firing me?' he stammered, his eyes filling with tears.

'No!' said Martin abruptly. 'I'm letting you go. Like a . . . dog. In the woods. Who's free now. But can't find his way home.'

'That really sounds like you're firing me!' cried Lou.

'OK, yes, I'm firing you.'

'You're firing me??!'

'No! I mean, yes. But I hope we can still be friends,' offered Martin meekly.

'We *are* friends. Imaginary friends!'

'Er, no. I meant more like . . . distant friends.

Friends who don't really see each other any more. Like pen pals. Who never write to each other.'

Loopy Lou gave a loud wail, then put his hands over his face and began to sob, completely distraught.

Martin had never seen a grown man cry before, apart from his dad who had sobbed like a baby when Ireland won the Eurovision Song Contest* in 1987. But he'd certainly never seen a grown imaginary man sob, and it wasn't a pleasant sight. So instead he looked away, to the window behind Lou, and found me peeping in.

I mouthed the words, 'How's it going?' through the glass.

Martin made a wobbly hand gesture – 'Not great.'

*EUROVISION SONG CONTEST – a showdown of Europe's musical titans who do battle with drum machines, shaved chests and a shedload of glitter.

I nodded sympathetically and made a gesture for him to hurry it along, tapping my watch and mouthing the word '*MacGyver*'.

'Just tell me why!' blubbed Lou, looking up from his sopping wet hands. 'WHY?!!'

'Er, no specific reason . . .' murmured Martin.

'Was I not wacky enough? Cos I can be way wackier! Want me to eat that bowl of sugar? Want me to punch the wall?'

'Er, no, thanks.'

But Lou had already jumped to his feet and clobbered the wall with his fist. He then howled in pain. 'OWOOOOOOOO!'

'Ah, Lou! That's the problem – you're *too* wacky.'

'I can be less wacky! I can be the most boring imaginary friend you ever had! Just please don't fire me. PLEASE!'

He banged on the table, but Martin just shook his head sadly. 'I'm sorry, Lou.'

Lou then flopped back down in his seat and began to sob again. 'I knew old Lou would mess it up! Old Loopy Loser!'

Martin leaned forward, feeling terrible. 'Look, Lou, I'll give you a great reference. You're a very talented imaginary friend. I'm sure you'll find another realsie.'

'No, I won't!' shouted Lou. 'Nobody wants me! Nobody loves Lou!'

'Ah, that's not true.'

'*You* don't want me!'

'Well, yes, that's true. But I'm sure someone else might.'

As Lou sobbed, he caught a glimpse of me looking through the window. He glared at me and I ducked out of sight. Lou then turned back to Martin angrily.

'Is it because of *him*?' he demanded, pointing a finger at the window accusingly.

'Who?' asked Martin.

'That lanky beardo! That Customer Service gombeen*! Is that who's replacing me?!'

'No, of course not.'

'Is that what you want, Martin? Some dum-dum in a cheap suit with a silly beard making stupid comments all day? Cos if that's what you want, then I can do that too! Better. I've got a lot of range, Marty.'

*GOMBEEN – Irish word for buffoon. Welsh word for fool. (Though the Welsh have many words for fool. Almost as many as the Eskimos have for snow, which is telling.)

Lou had a desperate look in his eyes and was squeezing Martin's hand tightly, which was freaking Martin out a little.

'I'm sorry, Lou,' said Martin finally. 'I have to go now.' He detached his hand from Lou's grip and stood up.

Lou glared at him. 'I thought we were gonna have a nice lunch! But you just brought me to a public place so I wouldn't make a scene – didn't you? Well, you were wrong about that, Marty Moo. Because I *will* make a scene!'

He jumped up on the table and started waving his arms about like a lunatic. 'Aaaarrrrgghhhh!'

Martin left a few coins on the table and hurried away, eager to escape the imaginary tantrum. He passed the waitress, who was just arriving with the drinks.

'Bye! Thanks!' he waved, and ran outside, leaving Loopy Lou wailing after him:

'Don't walk away from me, I'm not done crying yet!'

Outside the cafe, I was waiting for Martin. 'All done?' I asked chirpily.

But then Lou appeared at the door. 'This is all your fault, ya dingus! You're nothing but an imaginary home-wrecker! A realsie-robber!'

'Run!' cried Martin, and we sprinted away, leaving Lou hollering after us.

'MOO-MOO!! DON'T LEAVE ME!!'

It wasn't pretty, but Martin had done it. He'd fired old Lou. And I had to admit, I was pretty proud of the little dork as we dashed home through the rain to enjoy our last day of freedom. Which we spent wallpapering his schoolbooks.

## CHAPTER FIFTEEN
## FIRST DAY BACK

> **1st September**
> **Weather forecast: cloudy with a**
> **chance of rain. A good chance.**
> **A really good chance.**
> **Look, it's basically gonna rain all day.**

And so it was that I became the solitary IF of an idiot boy in the west of Ireland.

And then there we were, on our first walk to school. Him in his uniform, me in his head and hope in our hearts. And sand in our pockets. (Long story, don't ask.)

'I was thinking,' mused Martin (he would learn to embrace musing quite quickly), 'I was thinking . . . we could use this walk to and from school to catch up on the events of the day.

Perhaps I could regale* you with fantastical stories from my new class and you could tell me some of your stupid jokes or maybe dance a little.'

'Sounds ideal,' I said, though I knew the dancing bit was highly unlikely.

We walked on, both trying our best to think of something to say.

'It's hard to discuss the events of the day in the morning,' I said.

'Yes,' agreed Martin. 'Nothing's happened yet.'

'Well . . . what would you like the events of the day to be?'

'Today?' asked Martin, somewhat confused.

'Yes, I mean, are you excited about your first morning back?' I asked.

'Kinda. But it's at this stage of a new term that the nerves really kick in, CustServRep263. I'm wondering what the dynamics of the new class are going to be, if I'll get a decent desk position, whether the new teacher is going to

*REGALE - (*verb*) to amusingly retell a story. But a blustery version of it, which is pretty much full of hot air. Which is why it sounds like a second wind.

get my great jokes or will just think they're dumb and annoying like every other teacher has. And most importantly, how many people will notice I'm wearing last year's trousers, which are becoming dangerously short?'

'Yeah, there's certainly a lot to worry about there. Maybe we should just stay at home?' I offered.

'Yes, leaving the world of learning has certainly crossed my mind.'

'It'd be a brave move, buddy. Nobody would expect it.'

'That's true,' Martin agreed.

'I'll tell ya what – let's see how today goes, and consider living under a bridge from tomorrow on?'

Martin mulled over this suggestion for longer than I expected.

'Sounds good,' he said eventually. 'Let's give it a day.'

'Done,' I said, still thinking of cosy-looking bridges in the Boyle area.

'But I'll tell ya what I *am* excited about,' Martin went on, as he pulled a sheet of paper from his schoolbag. 'My new job.'

'Wow . . . ! If I'm honest, I'm not sure I was aware you were entering the work force, bud—'

'My new *class* job,' corrected Martin. 'At the start of every new term, pupils can apply for various integral classroom roles. Cloakroom monitor, blackboard cleaner, under-desk gum remover . . .'

'I get the idea,' I said. 'The teacher allocates jobs to you kids to cover the black hole between janitor's duties and "What can I be bothered to do myself?"'

'Exactamundo, CustServRep263!'

'So what's the plum job this year?'

'Well . . .' Martin straightened the sheet of paper. 'I'm putting myself forward for the pivotal role of "Sixth Class Goldfish Feeder" and I'm feeling pretty confident.' His tone was verging on smug.

He began to read: 'To whom it may concern . . .'

To whom it may concern (probably Mr Jackson),

I hereby apply for the post of chief feeder of Bob and Rob, your beloved goldfish.

I feel I am the perfect man for the position and will now outline the reasons why you should choose me and not smelly Alan or either of the brown nose* Joes.

    1. I am a lover of nature. All things nature I love. I would go so far as to say ... I'm a naturist**.

    2. I also have experience in the area of pet feeding. I once part-owned a gerbil with my sister Fidelma. The gerbil is no longer with us. This had almost nothing to do with my abilities as a feeder, but rather a bitter conflict over visiting rights, which led to the gerbil being released into the wild by my Dad.

Yours sincerely,

Martin Moone

---

**\*BROWN NOSE** – an expression referring to someone who gets the stuff you want. See also: *swot* and *fluke*.

**\*\*NATURIST** – lover of nature. Can also refer to old naked volleyball enthusiasts.

'That's pretty solid,' I said. 'Can't imagine what more they could be looking for than that.'

'Yup, I'm gonna feed the flip outta those little fish!'

'When do you find out if you've got the job?'

'It varies from teacher to teacher. Some of them can take days to decide on an applicant for a position as valuable as this. But now that I've thrown my hat in the ring, the verdict should come pretty quickly.' Martin scrumpled up his letter of intent and shoved it into his bag.

'Oh, that reminds me, Martin . . . I've gotta give you your realsie present for today.'

'A present?! I get a present every day?!!!' said Martin. 'I didn't know about that! That's the best news I've ever heard! Wow! Why did it take me this long to get an IF? This is the greatest day ever!'

'Oh . . . No. Not . . . Wait, it's just today, on my first day as your new IF. Not every day,' I explained awkwardly.

'Riiight,' said Martin, slightly disappointed.

'But it can be a good present, buddy. An imaginary can help a realsie choose one single item for when they start their lives together, like a dowry*.'

'So I can choose anything at all?'

'Yup, any *one* thing you can imagine, and that thing will leave the imaginary world and become real.'

'That's nuts!' squealed the excited boy.

'Like a monkey's breakfast,' I agreed.

'So . . . it could be a pot of gold?' Martin asked.

'I think leprechauns have the monopoly on the gold reserves, but I suppose it's possible.'

'A two-headed unicorn?'

'Pretty horny beasts, but sure, why not.'

'Wait!' Martin stopped. 'You're telling me that you could give me my two favourite words that when put together make an even better word?'

*DOWRY – a price a father pays for someone to take his smelly daughter off his hands.

169

'A SodaStream?' I guessed.

'No, a speedboat!'

'Yes, all you have to do is think really hard, imagine the thing you want, then click your fingers and it will become real. And you can keep it forever.'

'Holy schmoly, that's hard,' said the boy. 'I don't know if I can . . . Gosh. I mean . . . One thing! Forever. Amazing. But . . . it's a lot of pressure.'

'It is, buddy. That's the tricky bit.'

'Also, my imagination isn't the best.'

'You imagined me,' I remarked, a little hurt.

'That's true, I did imagine you. So maybe if I look into your imagination when I'm trying to imagine something, I'll think of something really amazing. Something that nobody else could imagine.'

'Let me get this straight. You're going to pick your present by staring at my mind?'

'That's the plan.'

I thought about the logic of that for quite a while.

'Sounds good!' was all that came to me.

'All righty then. Here we go . . .'

Martin took a step back and stared hard at my head. It felt as if his pale little eyes were burying through my hat, my hair, my skull and right into my thinking jelly. Then he closed his eyes and clicked his fingers, his wish made.

Instantly his wish came true. The thing that Martin saw when he stared at my head, then closed his eyes, had suddenly appeared.

It was a red woolly hat. He saw the red woolly hat on my head and couldn't imagine anything else. It was that simple. *He* was that simple.

'Where is it?!' asked the buffoon, excited.

'You're wearing it, ya gombeen.'

Martin felt the top of his head, where a red woolly hat now sat. He yanked it off and stared glumly at his shoddy IF gift.

'Right,' he whispered, clearly a little disappointed. 'Well . . . we'd better . . .

get a wiggle on.' And he forced his hat back on to his unhappy head.

We moved off together, both red-faced and red-hatted.

'How long is this walk anyway?' I asked, already tired.

'It's just over eight minutes.'

'What a pain.'

'I know,' agreed Martin. 'If only we could come up with some kind of genius shortcut that would allow me to stay longer in bed.'

'Yes!' I agreed.

We stopped for a moment to have a little think. Nothing came.

'Not to worry,' Martin chirped. 'We'll think of something when our brains wake up.'

'Yeah, buddy,' I said. 'Thinking this early is clearly dangerous.'

## CHAPTER SIXTEEN
## A NEW CLASS

As we finally reached the school gates, Martin's
dozy eyes spotted the Bonner brothers, an
identical pair of bomber-jacket wearing bullies.
Martin tensed, readying himself for some
manly running-away. But thankfully they were
too busy rewriting last year's graffiti on to
the newly painted gate to notice him, and he
managed to sneak by unharmed. But his sleepy
brain was then sharply awoken by a firm flick
to his left ear lobe.

'Yowchh!' he yelped, more high-pitched than
he'd have liked.

'A flick to the ear for a happy school year!'
chirped Padraic, now walking alongside him.
Padraic's round little face was beaming with
the radiance of a recently released convict –

especially when compared to the parade of gloomy-guts that passed by the boys on their sad march into St Brendan's* school yard.

'Hey P-Nog, you're perky for a Monday morning.'

'We're back at school! I'm free! No more sewage shovelling, basket weaving or lamb wrangling for nine months. Speaking of baskets . . . Are you aware your mother's knitting basket has fallen on your head, Martin?' Padraic added, not joking.

'Oh, this?' Martin sighed, pointing at his new scalp attire. 'No, this is my realsie gift.'

'Ohhh, I like it. A humble choice. Fair play to you. It's very . . . red, isn't it?'

'Why, what did you choose when you got yours?' Martin asked.

'Well . . . now mine feels a bit silly.'

'Go on, what did you get as your realsie gift?'

*ST BRENDAN - patron saint of bongo players. And lost cats.

'Er, South America. I own that continent now.'

We stood in silence for a moment, realizing our realsie gift had been trumped somewhat.

'Anyhoo . . .' Padraic muttered, breaking the tension, '. . . let's get in there and grab our new seats before all the good desks get took.'

As Padraic skipped away, Martin turned to me and eyed my guilty hat.

'I'd say Argentina would be very hard to keep clean,' I offered.

Martin rolled his eyes and joined the back of the gloomy-guts parade.

As far as desks go, it's all about location, location, location. You want to be close to the door, the toilet and the window that opens, but very, very far from Smelly Simon Egan. Padraic had managed to pinch a pretty decent spot for them both behind Lucky Larry Loughran and Alan Something. (Alan's surname wasn't actually 'something', but his real surname was long and hard to pronounce, so he'd been known to the class as Alan Something for five years now.)

Martin and Padraic were settling nicely into their new seats as they watched the procession of classmates filter through the door.

'I hear Dominic Geraghty lost a toe to an infection he picked up at the county swimming pool,' Padraic whispered, as the boys watched a young lad hobble through the door.

'I warned him to wear swimming socks, but would he listen?' snorted Martin.

The boys gossiped their way through student after student, until eventually a slightly older face swept through the doorway.

'No way!' Martin hushed.

'Declan Mannion!' exclaimed Padraic, but quietly. (Which is quite hard to do.)

The boys stared at the leather-jacketed, slick-haired teenager who breezed through the classroom like a spotty rock star. He was casually swinging what appeared to be a set of car keys around his pinky.

'I can't believe he still hasn't graduated! How many years can they hold him back?' Padraic whispered.

'I don't know. A friend of Fidelma's was in London last summer and swore she saw him driving a bus,' Martin added.

'My dad told me Declan was a drummer in a band he liked in the seventies.'

As the boys shared Mannion memories, Declan suddenly stopped and stared right at them. His eyes were grey and piercing like the corner of an old gate. 'What are ye two ladies gawkin' at?'

The boys froze.

'Don't be intimidated, Martin,' I said.

'Say something witty but profound* to let him know who's boss.'

'I always wear swimming socks. Just in case,' Martin said sheepishly.

Perfect, I thought. Perfect.

\*PROFOUND – the opposite of anti-found. Means insightful\*\*.

\*\*INSIGHTFUL – the opposite of outsightful.

It was hard to tell what Declan made of this confession, but the moment of confusion was broken suddenly as Mr Jackson, the sixth-class teacher, plonked through the door.

'All right now, sit, sit, sit. Let's get this over with.'

I wasn't sure what he meant. Get what over with? The year? We'd barely started.

'Welcome, welcome, blah, blah, fire exits there and there, blah, blah, blah . . .'

He had a rugged, deep voice, like a neglected well. His face was stubbled, which seemed destined to reach 'beard' status by the day's end. Being the bearer of a fine beard myself, I liked his style.

'Take your usual seat, Declan, if you will.'

'Will do, Jermaine,' Declan replied as he took the back desk to himself.

'First things first. Let's get these class tasks handed out so.'

Martin had left his application letter on Mr Jackson's desk and smiled hopefully at his new teacher. Mr Jackson allocated job after job to seemingly uninterested folk. Blackboard Cleaner, Window Closer, Marble Gatherer . . . Until finally . . .

'All right, who wants to be class Goldfish Feeder?'

Martin's hand shot up, a lone paw in a kennel of bored puppies.

'Grand,' sighed Mr Jackson. 'Moone can be this year's—'

A delicate knock on the classroom door stopped the teacher in his tracks. Martin watched as in stepped an unfamiliar face. A new boy!

'Ah!' Mr Jackson exclaimed. 'There you are, Trevor. Did you get lost?'

'Sorry I'm late, teacher. I dropped my pencil case in a urinal,' Trevor murmured.

The class giggled as Padraic turned to Martin and whispered, 'I've done that.'

'Class, this is Trevor, he's joining us from the big smoke in Dublin. Say, "Hello."'

'Hello, Trevor!' the class replied unenthusiastically as Trevor managed an awkward wave in response.

'Trevor,' continued the teacher, 'sit down in that spare seat by Alan Something. And why don't *you* take the role of Goldfish Feeder this year?'

'NOOOOO!' Martin screamed. Inside.

He couldn't believe it. So close. He turned to Padraic, disgusted by this sudden turn of events.

'How could the new kid take my job?! I deserved my chance. Look at him, with his clean face and his spit-less back. Makes me sick!'

Padraic nodded sadly. 'His uniform looks like it's the first year he's worn it, the fancy flute.'

'I've earned my stripes,' Martin went on. 'That tool won't know what to do with those goldfish. Mark my words, Padraic, Bob and Rob will be dead within the month.'

'Oh . . .' Mr Jackson started. 'And, Moone . . .

I need someone to clear up the litter in the yard after school. Want to be Garbage Prefect?'

I looked at Martin, waiting for his groan of discontent. His hopes shattered, his dream job pinched by a big-city blow-in*. He thought for a moment, weighing up his response.

'Cool!' he said happily.

Prefect, I thought. Prefect.

*BIG-CITY BLOW-IN – someone from another town. Alternative term: *city farter*.

# CHAPTER SEVENTEEN
## BULLIES

I scanned the long grass at my feet and soon
spied an empty Monster Mulch* packet trodden
into the sodden ground.

'More rubbish over here, Martin!' I yelled,
and he bounded over with his plastic sack.

'Great stuff!' he smiled happily, plucking the
litter out of the muck with his filthy fingers.
He popped it into his bag, which was already
half full of popsicle sticks, apple cores, chewing
gum, empty cans, sweet wrappers, Yop bottles,
and half-eaten sandwiches that he'd already
gathered up.

'This school of ours is a rubbish bonanza,'

*MONSTER MULCH – monster-shaped crisps. Not
to be confused with Tayto-Gaters which are
crisp-shaped monsters.

he beamed. 'Another hour or so, and we should have a full sack!'

'Another hour?!' I groaned. 'I can't believe Mr Jackson is making us do this just because we . . .' I tried to remember what we'd done to get ourselves into this scrape. 'Wait, why are we being punished?'

'We're not being punished, pal. We're being rewarded! With the plum post of Garbage Prefect!'

'That's right!' I said enthusiastically. Then wavered a bit. 'Although . . . there doesn't seem to be a *huge* amount of "plum"-ness going on here. I mean, apart from that rotten plum we found.'

Martin held up the bag. 'It's really perked up the pong, hasn't it?'

'Oh, it's definitely been the high point of the day, buddy. But I can't help thinking that being employed feels a lot like being punished.'

Martin shrugged, his enthusiasm undampened. 'Well, this might not have the glamour of Goldfish Feeder. But we've got a job, CustServRep263! We're employed!' He gestured at the other kids who were heading home or loitering at the school gates. 'Not like those useless slackers.'

'Yeah! Flippin' wasters. Enjoying their stupid freedom.'

We could see Declan Mannion puffing on a cigar and reading out the names of greyhounds to one of his minions*, who was scribbling them down.

'Not even Declan Mannion got a job,' bragged Martin smugly.

'Well, he looks pretty jealous all right. I bet he'd do anything to swap his career as a professional gambler to be a Garbage Prefect.'

We watched Declan peel off a few ten-pound notes from a wad of cash and hand them to his lackey, who sprinted away to the betting shop.

*MINIONS - a motley crew of pre-teen boys, often used to carry out boring tasks, like fetching a newspaper or stealing a car.

Then Declan took a last puff of his cigar and flicked the butt in Martin's direction.

'Many thanks, Declan!' Martin waved happily.

But Declan didn't even notice him as he swaggered away.

'He's so sophisticated,' marvelled Martin.

We ambled across the grass to bag the butt, but before we could get there, Martin suddenly came to a stop, staring at the ground.

'O.M.F.G.!' he cried out. 'Open My Flippin' Guts!'

He had spotted a small brown bird lying on the ground.

I crouched down to peer at it closer.

'Easy, CustServRep263. Don't startle it.'

'It looks pretty startled alright,' I whispered, staring at the little chaffinch that was lying completely still.

'It must be injured,' said Martin. 'We've got to help it. We've got to nurse it back to health.'

I looked at him blankly. 'Should we give it some of the plum?'

Martin crouched down beside me and whispered to the bird, 'Do you want some plum, little one?'

But the bird didn't respond. She was certainly a quiet little gal.

Martin picked up the chaffinch gently. 'You'll be back on your feet in no time, my lady.'

He stroked its little feathers gently, but the bird remained quite stiff and silent. He leaned closer, then looked at me, concerned. 'Her breathing is becoming faint.'

It seemed to me that her breathing was very faint indeed. Non-existent in fact. 'All right, well, you know what to do, buddy,' I told him. 'Don't be shy.'

Martin nodded, understanding. Then he puckered up his lips and breathed into its little beak, giving it the kiss of life.

There he was, giving mouth-to-mouth to a (deceased) chaffinch, when who should walk by but the school bullies, the Bonner brothers. This wasn't the most ideal moment to be seen by anyone, but particularly the Bonner twins, who were clearly unfamiliar with CPR (Chaffinch or Pigeon Resuscitation).

'Ugh!' yelled Jonner Bonner. 'Moone's shifting* a dead bird!'

'Yuck!' added Conor Bonner.

'No, lads. Woah!' I said, as they advanced menacingly. 'That's not shifting. There was no tongue there!'

'It's medical shifting!' beseeched Martin.

But the Bonners had already grabbed the comatose** chaffinch and tossed her aside.

*SHIFTING – an Irish term for French kissing (*see* Chapter Twenty-Two), so-called because Irish tongues are particularly shifty and should never be trusted.

**COMATOSE – as close to death as sleeping gets.

They then upended Martin's schoolbag, dumping out his wallpapered books.

'Argh! My lovely books!' he wailed.

They took his sack and emptied it over his head.

'Argh! My lovely rubbish!'

And doled out two dead arms.

'Argh! My lovely arms!'

With businesslike efficiency, they then moved to his rear and proceeded to give him a wedgie.

'Come on, CustServRep263! Do something!' Martin called to me.

I looked at him, confused. 'Do . . . what exactly?'

'Help me! Don't just stand there!'

'Erm . . .' I frowned, a little puzzled. 'I think you might have misinterpreted my abilities in this area, buddy.'

'In what wa-OWWW! MY FLIPPIN' BUMHOLE!' he wailed, as the Bonners yanked the back of his underpants up towards his armpits.

'Well, I'm really more of an advisor,' I
explained, 'a confidante. A *consiglieri**, if
you will. But I suppose the main downside in
situations like this is that I *am* imaginary. So I
can't really intervene.'

'Right,' grunted Martin through gritted
teeth. 'That's disappointing.'

'Yeah. We probably should have clarified
that earlier.'

The Bonners were now working his upper
body, smacking Martin with his own arms. 'Stop
hitting yourself, stop hitting yourself, stop
hitting yourself!'

'Maybe you could *imagine* yourself not
getting hurt?' I suggested.

'I'm doing that.'

'Is it working?'

'Yeah, I think it is!' said Martin hopefully.
But then winced with pain. 'No – actually –

*CONSIGLIERI* – an advisor to a Mafia boss.
Also, my favourite chocolate-pasta dish.

I just went numb there for a bit.'

'Who ya talking to, idiot?' demanded Jonner Bonner.

'No one,' squeaked Martin meekly.

'We like to dole out our beatings in silence.'

'Yeah!' barked Conor Bonner. 'Shut up so we can bully you in peace!'

'Of course. Will do. Sorry, lads,' apologized Martin.

Jonner Bonner looked at Conor Bonner. 'Right. Now where were we?'

Conor Bonner frowned. He was the slightly more dim-witted Bonner. Which was saying something. 'Er, we saw him shiftin' a dead bird, then . . . we basically attacked him.'

'After that. Have we done Chinese burns* yet?'

*CHINESE BURN – a violent massage of the forearm that turns the skin red-hot. In ancient China this was done to warm pots of tea.

'I can't remember. To be honest, I wasn't really paying attention.'

Jonner Bonner noticed that Martin's underpants were pulled halfway up his back. 'Looks like we did the wedgie. Shall we go from there?'

Conner Bonner seemed hesitant. 'I dunno. I've kind of lost my flow now.'

'Me too,' admitted Jonner Bonner.

Martin brightened. 'Well, maybe we should just leave it there then . . . ?'

'Let's just start again,' said Jonner Bonner finally.

'Good plan!' His brother grinned.

Martin groaned, 'Oh balls.'

'Moone's shifting a dead bird!' yelled the Bonners, and re-deadened his already dead arms.

## CHAPTER EIGHTEEN
## THE BIG ONE-TWO

Martin's troubles with the Bonner brothers continued for the next few weeks and were no less troublesome by the eve of his twelfth birthday. Almost every day, as Martin carried out his duties of Garbage Prefect, the twins would swagger over with their identical black bomber jackets and their identical stupid faces, like a zippered-up two-headed bully beast. And almost every day they'd torment him with every trick in the bully book – from Wet Willies* to Noggin Nuggies** to Nipple Cripples***, all carried out on their infamous tickle-rack.

*WET WILLIE – licking your finger and sticking it in someone's ear. Not as pleasant as it sounds.

**NOGGIN NUGGIE – A nuggie on your noggin.

***NIPPLE CRIPPLE – the squeezing of the male nipple. Let's face it, male nipples are fairly pointless, so at least bullies have found a use for them.

Once litter-picking and bullying were done
for the day, we strolled home together, and I
tried not to let that dumb duo dampen Martin's
excitement for his big day.

'I can't believe you're turning twelve!' I
beamed at him enthusiastically. 'I wish we
could just go to sleep right now so tomorrow
would finally be here.'

'Ahh, the glorious sixteenth,' Martin smiled
as we ambled along. 'October's mightiest day.'

'I bet your family are all at home right now
frantically wrapping your presents!'

'Haha. Yeah,' chuckled Martin. He thought about this for a moment. 'Actually that doesn't sound very likely, to be honest. They don't have the greatest track record of quality-gift-giving.'

'Oh? How do you mean?'

'Well, let's see. Last year, Mam and Dad gave me a hoop.'

'A hoop? Like a hula hoop?'

'No no, a metal hoop. Dad said it was a basketball hoop. But it wasn't a basketball hoop. It was just a hoop. I think it might have been part of a lamp shade.'

'So what did you do with it?'

'I just . . . rolled it around for a while,' he said sadly. 'My other presents included a glass of milk from Fidelma, a "nightmare catcher" from Trisha, which she'd made herself—'

'A nightmare catcher? Like a dream catcher*?'

*DREAM CATCHER – a Native American contraption that you hang over your bed to catch dreams. My one only ever caught dust clumps and a small moth – so I guess that's what dreams look like!

195

'Similar, yes. But for nightmares. Which Trisha thinks are more fun. And from Sinead I got a sock puppet.'

'Hey, that's not too bad,' I said cheerfully. 'Sock puppets are fun!'

'Sock puppets *are* fun. But this was just a sock, which she said was a puppet. There was no face on it or anything. It was just a manky old sock. "Try it," said Mam. "Try out your new sock puppet." "Try it," they all said. "Give us a puppet show, Martin." They made me put my hand inside one of Sinead's stinky, fungusy socks and perform for them like a smelly sock-wearing dancing monkey. So yes, that was my last birthday.'

'Yeesh.' I winced. 'Well, I guess they can't do much worse than that.'

'Exactly!' said Martin as he reached the top of the hill. 'That's why tomorrow's going to be so great! It's all uphill from here!' he said optimistically, and then proceeded to walk downhill.

'Marty Moo?! Is that you?' came a wretchedly recognizable voice. There was a rustling beside us, and suddenly Loopy Lou's balding head protruded through the hedge.

'Argh!' yelped Martin, jumping back. Lou's entrances had a habit of scaring him, but Lou just smiled his silly smile and Martin tried to look less alarmed. 'I mean, er . . . Hi, Lou.'

'Hi!' said Lou.

He then noticed me standing beside him and his smile wavered a bit. 'Oh. Hello,' he said curtly.

'Hello there.' I smiled back.

There was a pause as we all looked at each other. We hadn't seen Lou since Martin fired him at the cafe and I had to admit this was feeling a teeny bit awkward.

'You're . . . looking well,' said Martin. Which was a lie. Lou wasn't looking well at all. He looked quite grubby, with smudges of dirt on his face, and a little cut on his chin. One of his coat pockets was ripped, and there were a number of small twigs in his hair.

'What are you doing in the hedge?' I asked curiously.

'Ah, nothing much. Just . . . having a bit of Lou-time. Hedges are a lot more comfortable than you'd think. *Way* nicer than slurry pits. That's a facteroo, Marty Moo!'

'Are they not a bit scratchy?' I asked.

'That's the best part! Whenever something

starts to itch, I just wiggle around and the brambles do the scratching for me!'

'Sounds handy all right.'

Martin gave Lou a sympathetic smile. 'Well, I'm glad you're doing better now, Lou.'

'Oh, I'm right as raindrops, Marty! Getting fired was the best thing that ever happened to Lou! No more realsies to boss me around. I'm free and easy!'

'So no one's picked you to be their imaginary friend?'

'Absolutely not. Not a whiff. But I'm not worried, Marty. Old Lou always gets by. It's just a dry patch. I still do some odd-jobs every now and then. Last week I got some part-time work as a daydream. And before that I did a few hours as a passing thought. So I'm keeping busy – yes, I am! And besides – I'm out in the open, getting lots of fresh air. I'm living the dream!'

'You're living in a hedge,' I said bluntly.

Lou prickled a bit, glaring at me.

'Well, it was lovely to see ya, Lou,' said

Martin, eager to move on.

'Wait, wait! I got a birthday present for you, Marty.'

Martin's face lit up. 'A birthday present?'

'Never had a chance to give you your realsie gift. So I thought I'd save it for your birthday!'

Lou reached into the hedge and pulled out a large box that was wrapped in a bow. He handed it to the delighted boy, who shook it, but the box seemed empty.

'What's in it?' Martin enquired.

Lou leaned closer, with a mysterious look in his eyes. 'Whatever you imagin—'

'We've already done this, Lou,' I interrupted impatiently. 'He knows how realsie presents work.'

Lou glared at me, annoyed. 'Do you have to always be such a party pooper, poop-face?'

I touched my brown beard a little self-consciously. 'Well, at least I don't live in a hedge. Ya flippin' hedge . . . hog!'

Lou stared at me coldly for a few moments.

He then turned back to Martin and resumed his act. 'Whatever you imagine to be in it!' he cried mysteriously.

Martin beamed with excitement. 'Well, I'll tell you what I'm NOT going to do, and that's imagine another flippin' hat! Hahaha!'

I joined in his laughter, 'Hahaha! Could you imagine that?'

'I know!' he laughed, 'Imagine if I imagined another flippin' hat and then clicked my fingers –' he chuckled, clicking his fingers.

Then he stopped laughing and suddenly had a worried look.

'Oh balls.'


A little later, Martin was walking glumly up the Moone driveway wearing two hats, one tucked under the other.

'You could have imagined anything, Martin,' I complained, as I trudged slowly alongside him. 'Rocket-boots. A chocolate fountain. A sister-less family.'

Martin shook his head in despair. 'It's just really hard not to think about hats when you're trying not to think about hats.'

He had a point, I suppose. If I tell you not to think about hats, aren't you going to think about not thinking about hats?

OK, let's try it. Don't think about hats. Starting . . . NOW!

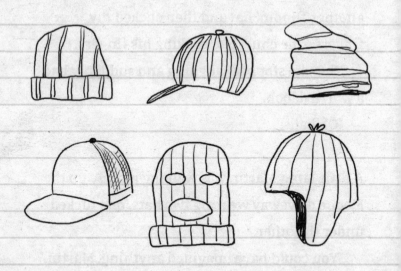

You're not doing great. Focus! Just think about nothing but NO hats.

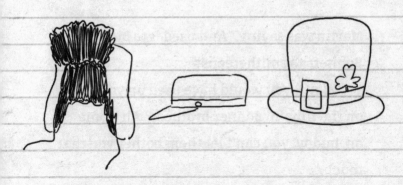

No hats. No hats. No hats. No hats. No hats.
No hats. No hats. No hats. No hats. No hats.

So, how did that work out for ya?

Yeah, that's what I thought.

OK, back to Martin, who's blathering on about something.

'I could have wished for a submarine,'

Martin was saying, 'And used it to blow the Bonners to smithereens!'

'Wait – you would have used up your wish on the flippin' Bonner brothers? Ah, come on, buddy, you can't let them bother you that much.'

'Yeah, I guess you're right, pal. I mean, there's only seven more years of school. If we subtract holidays, that's only about . . . four million days of bullying. Wow. That's a lot of wedgies.'

'Well, at least you've got your maths skills to help you get by.'

Martin sighed gloomily and I couldn't help but feel sorry for the little idiot.

'Come on. Chin up, buddy. You can't let a little rough-housing dampen your spirits. Remember, tomorrow's your big day. Things get way easier when you turn twelve.'

Martin brightened up again. 'Yeah. The big one-two!'

'That's right,' I said, as we approached the

house. 'I bet they're in there right now planning out your party as we speak.'

Martin threw open the front door and strolled inside jauntily.

'I'm home!' he called out. 'Better hide my presents!'

Sinead walked by, glaring at him. 'Mam says you were a mistake.'

Martin's shoulders sagged as she swaggered off.

'Not a mistake!' I yelled at her. 'An accident!'

# CHAPTER NINETEEN
## BIRTHDAY BOY

> **Forecast: a deluge of birthday presents in the morning, followed by a smattering of cards and well-wishing throughout the day. Chance of cake: 83%**

**16th October.** Birthday of:

Oscar Wilde – poet, playwright, and snappy
   dresser.

Michael Collins – freedom-fighter and
   politician.

Martin Moone – local dopey-headed doodler.


The Glorious Sixteenth had arrived at last
and the sun was streaming through Martin's
bedroom window – which was a strange way
for the day to begin. The sun wasn't in the
habit of 'streaming' in Boyle. It tended to cower

bashfully behind rain clouds, desperate to stay out of sight, like a naked nun. But here it was, blazing over the Moone home, as bold and brassy as a naked nun.

Clearly this day was going to be different.

The sunlight warmed Martin's face as he lay sprawled across his bed, fast asleep, mouth agape, drooling a small pool of saliva on to his pillow. Eventually he gave a snort, stirred awake and slowly opened his eyes to see my handsome face right beside him, beaming at him excitedly. I was crouched by his bed in a state of cat-like readiness and now leaped to my feet.

'Happy birthday!' I hollered.

Martin seemed confused for a moment. 'Birthday . . . ?' he murmured sleepily – then suddenly sat up. 'It's my birthday!!' he cried with glee.

He hopped to his feet and danced on his bed, singing tunelessly, 'It's my birthday! It's my birthday!'

I tried to join him on the bed, but my legs weren't working properly after all that cat-like crouching. 'Argh! Cramp!' I wailed, clutching my thigh.

He stopped dancing. 'How long were you crouched there?'

'I dunno. A few hours? Imaginary friends are supposed to be the first ones to wish their realsies a happy birthday, so I didn't want to miss it.'

Martin smiled, touched. 'Aww. Thanks, beard-face.'

He hopped to the floor. 'Right, let's get this party started. Bring forth my gifts!'

I grinned and called behind me in a Shakespearean voice. 'Bring forth his gifts!'

After a pause, I turned back and saw that he was looking at me expectantly.

'Oh. You mean *me*? You didn't really expect me to buy you something, did you? You pay me in crisps, Martin. Imaginary crisps.'

'Fair enough.' Martin nodded. 'To the

gift-atorium!' he cried.

'Do you mean the kitchen?'

'I mean wherever the gift-givers are! And yes, that's probably the kitchen!'

Martin skipped out of his room and down the hallway, embracing his great new age with optimism and gay abandon. Which he abandoned very quickly.

His sisters were sitting at the kitchen table, but there was no mountain of presents before them. The only 'gift' to be seen was a cheap-looking pen lying in front of Sinead on an unwrapped square of wrapping paper.

'A biro?' frowned Martin.

'Cool,' said Sinead with relief, as she handed him the pen. 'Don't have to finish wrapping it now.'

Martin regarded the biro with dismay. Half the ink was gone and the lid was indented with Sinead's tooth-marks. He sighed inwardly, then turned to his middle sister, Trisha, who was slouched beside Sinead.

'I already gave you your present,' she reminded him.

'Yes, you . . . did,' confirmed Martin, looking at the ragged piece of cloth she'd tied around his wrist the previous night.

'What did you call this thing again, Trish?'

'Did I call it something?' she said cluelessly.

'A . . . cravat?' he offered.

'Sure, it's a cravat. Why not? Happy birthday.'

'Yeah. Thanks again,' he said, through gritted teeth.

Martin then turned to Fidelma, who smiled at him warmly. 'Ta-daa!' his eldest sister sang, handing him a card.

'This better be vouchers, Delma,' Martin warned her.

'It is. Sort of.'

Hoping for the best, Martin opened the card.

He was not impressed.

Dear Martin,
i ou one present.
Love,
xxx
Fidelma

'I always think your birthday's in August,' she said with a confused expression.

'So why don't you give me what you got me in August?'

'I just did,' she said with a shrug.

This wasn't the turnaround that Martin had been hoping for. He'd really thought that his family were going to surprise him this year. But he was starting to resign himself to the fact that this birthday was going to be just as awful as all the others – when something amazing happened.

'And now for the main event!' cried Liam,

who had snuck into the room behind him. 'Happy birthday, pal!'

Martin turned to see his dad holding up a large, brightly wrapped package.

I'd been quietly sipping my tea and almost did a spit-take* when I saw the size of the gift. This was no hoop. And although I didn't want to get my hopes up, it did look suspiciously bicycle-shaped.

'No!' I gasped. 'Surely they haven't got you something decent!'

Martin dashed forward and began to attack the wrapping paper, but I shook my head, not willing to believe it.

'It must be a bicycle-shaped sock,' I told him. 'Or a bicycle-shaped toilet brush. Or a bicycle-shaped kick in the arse!'

*SPIT-TAKE – an explosive power shower from your mouth. Usually occurs when you see something surprising or hilarious just after you've taken a drink. Definitely the most fun way to drink a glass of water. Not including sticking a straw up your nose.

But through the half-ripped paper, Martin could make out a wheel and part of the frame.

'Wow!' he exclaimed. 'It's a bicycle-shaped bicycle!'

'Don't get too excited,' grunted Sinead. 'It's only from Readybix.'

Martin and I looked at each other in amazement. Every morning at breakfast we'd stare at pictures of the Readybix bike, read about the special offer and imagine ourselves cruising around town on it just like the Readybix Kid*. But we'd never expected to

*READYBIX KID – the Readybix Kid was originally played by a blond boy called Alfie Sewell from Berkshire in England, but after publicly admitting that he wouldn't eat a bowl of Readybix even if his life depended on it, he was replaced by the Readybix Monkey, Ready Eddie. The much-loved ape would go on to represent Readybix for almost two decades, until he eventually died after falling off a chandelier in a gentlemen's club** in Leeds.

*GENTLEMEN'S CLUB – a club where gentlemen go to take a break from being gentlemen.

see one in the flesh! Could this really be the Readybix bike??

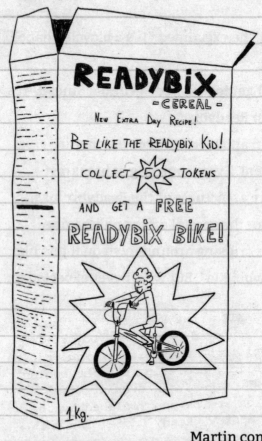

Martin continued to wrench off the wrapping paper, and sure enough, there was the Readybix logo, painted boldly along the crossbar.

'Yes! It's the Readybix bike!' he squealed, barely containing his excitement.

He turned to his mam and dad, genuinely touched. 'Thank you! This is amazing!'

Liam and Debra smiled, a little taken aback by his gratitude. They weren't used to such emotion from their children.

'But how?' asked Martin. 'You needed fifty tokens!'

Debra gave a coy smile and strolled across the kitchen. 'Well, let's just say –' she opened two cupboards to reveal stacks of Readybix boxes piled high – 'I hope you all like Readybix!'

There was a collective groan from the three sisters.

'Nobody likes Readybix, Mam,' complained Fidelma. 'That's why they have to give away free bikes.'

I had to agree with her. 'I'm not eating that turf,' I muttered to Martin.

'Well, your father can't eat it all,' Debra told them. 'Everyone has to pitch in.'

Liam had a half-eaten bowl in his hands and was looking a bit ill. 'She's right – six bowls a day is all I can handle. We need the digestive systems of the full Team Moone on this.'

The sisters rolled their eyes and begrudgingly began to pour themselves bowls of Readybix as Martin gazed adoringly at his new bike.

'Best. Present. Ever,' he murmured happily.

# CHAPTER TWENTY
## BROTHERS GRIMM

That morning, Martin cycled his new Readybix bike all over Boyle. I hopped on the back and we rode across Abbeytown Bridge, past the crumbling ruin of the abbey, down Shop Street and into the centre of town. It was busy enough for a Saturday morning and we waved at everyone, in the friendliest mood of our lives.

'Good morning, townspeople!' Martin called, waving cheerfully.

'Check it, yo!' I yelled at them, making ill-advised hip-hop gestures with my hands.

A few of the bemused locals waved back at Martin, but the younger ones just stared jealously at his new bike, which was exactly what we wanted.

'That's right, losers! It's the Readybix bike!

Read it and weep!' I taunted, gesturing at the shiny Readybix logo on the crossbar.

We cycled down Bridge Street, where we passed Trevor eating a bag of Monster Mulch.

'Hey, new kid!' called Martin, and Trevor waved back, delighted that somebody knew who he was, sort of. 'All your money couldn't buy *this* sweet ride, Richy McRich!'

'Yeah!' I yelled. 'All your money could only buy the tokens! And then you'd have to send them away! And probably wait two to three weeks for delivery, sucker!'

On Main Street we passed Declan Mannion, who was sipping an espresso* and reading a copy of the *Racing Past***.

**\*ESPRESSO** – a tiny coffee served in a miniature cup. It's basically coffee for elves. Although if you ever see an elf drinking one, then stand well back, as it tends to make them dangerously farty.

**\*\*RACING PAST** – a form guide for horse-and-hound racing. This publication will inform you if your beast has ever won, lost or stopped mid-race to do a wee.

218

'Hi, Declan!' called Martin. 'Check out my new wheels!'

Declan glanced up and frowned, as if he'd never seen Martin before in his life.

'I'm in your class!' called Martin helpfully as he rode off. But Declan just shrugged blankly and returned to the greyhound news.

We swung a left on Patrick Street and soon left Boyle behind. We cycled off into the countryside, past fields and farms, hills and hedgerows. We were now in a distant land known as Just Outside Boyle and were soon weaving down the winding, rubbishy road towards Padraic's house.

As we approached, we spotted Padraic atop a ladder. He was holding an armful of twigs and was hard at work thatching* the roof.

'Hi, Padraic!' called Martin.

Padraic smiled brightly. 'Happy birthday, Mar—'

*THATCHING – the process of tying a bush to your roof.

But when he saw Martin's new bike he stopped, stunned. He dumped the twigs, shimmied down the ladder and came charging out on to the road just as we were passing.

'Woah!' he cried, in awe, 'the Readybix bike! Radical!*'

Martin kept pedalling and Padraic raced alongside us, trying to keep up. He wasn't the most athletic sort of lad, and his face was soon glistening with sweat.

'Any chance . . .' he gasped, 'I could . . . have a go on it?'

'Hmm?' asked Martin, pretending that he hadn't quite heard him.

'Faster, Martin,' I urged. 'Faster!'

I wasn't about to let Padraic's tubby frame weaken the Readybix suspension.

*RADICAL! – word of exclamation popular with schoolboys in the 1980s. Other big hits that decade included 'Bodacious!', 'Extreme!', and 'Nud!' As in, 'That's totally nud!'

'I said,' panted Padraic, 'any chance . . .
I could . . .'

But Martin was freewheeling downhill now, leaving Padraic clutching his pudgy sides, heaving for breath as we soared off.

Martin pedalled up and down the country lanes with the wind in his hair and the sun on his face. We passed a farmer with a dog and Martin waved. 'Hello, Mr Farmer! Hello, Mr Farmer's Dog!'

We passed some cows.

'Hiya, cows!' waved Martin.

'Mooooone!' mooed a friendly heifer. 'Love the new bike!'

We passed some pigs.

'How are ye, pigs?!' I called.

'Hey, it's the Readybix Boys! Give us some Readybix!'

They tore after us, but we just laughed as we zoomed away.

We then looped back towards town, and we weren't far from Boyle when we spotted

a figure squatting at the side of the road. At
first we thought it was a tramp – Right Beside
Boyle is littered with them – but as we got closer
we realized it was Loopy Lou. He was even
grubbier than last time, his clothes were more
tattered and he was cooking one of his large red
shoes over a campfire.

'Hi, Lou!' called Martin, as we rolled towards him.

'Don't stop, Martin,' I whispered, and he kept pedalling slowly.

'Hey, it's the birthday boy!' Lou smiled as he jumped to his feet, holding the stick with his half-cooked shoe on the end of it. 'Oooh, me likey the new bikey!'

'Thanks, Lou!' Martin smiled.

'No touchy though, yeah?' I warned Lou, not wanting his grubby mitts marking the paintwork.

Lou bounded around us, admiring the bike. 'Oh, it's a real beaut, Marty!' he cooed. 'All shiny like a jellyfish's belly. It's even got that new-bike smell! Like a jellyfish's belly! I don't suppose you got any jellyfish, Marty? I so hungry.'

'Hungry?' I scoffed. 'You've got a whole shoe there!'

Lou gave me one of his cold looks.

'Did you move out of your hedge?' asked Martin, as we cycled slowly along the road.

'Booted out, more like,' complained Lou. 'Evicted! You ever been evicted? It's a nasty business, Marty.'

'Evicted? By who?'

'A bunch of damn dirty ducks. Quack! Quack! Quack! Pecking at me day and night. Quack! Quack! Quack! Quack! Quack!'

'Sounds like it's *you* that's quacking up, Lou.' I grinned.

Martin chuckled, and Lou bristled with anger.

'I'm not quacking up! And if I am, it's your fault!' he yelled, jabbing a filthy finger at me. 'I'm out on the street cos of you, you stupid clerk! You're just like those damn ducks! Quack! Quack! Quack! It should be me on that Readybix bike, not you!'

'Let's roll, Martin,' I whispered, and he quickened our pace. 'Enjoy your shoe, ya looper!'

Lou was still running alongside us awkwardly, with one shoe on his foot and the other on his stick. 'You're not even a proper imaginary friend!' he yelled. 'You're a nobody! An imaginary pencil-pusher! You're an imposter!'

'Yeah?' I scoffed. 'What are ya gonna do about it?'

'Oh, I'm gonna do something, don't you worry! This isn't over, lanky! You've made a powerful enemy, my friend!'

'So I'm your friend?'

'I mean, you've made a powerful friend, my enemy!'

'So you're my powerful friend?'

'I mean – Dammit!'

I guffawed with laughter and we left him eating our dust.

We cruised back through town for one last glory lap and had just sailed across the little green bridge when we suddenly came face to face with the Bonners.

Martin squeezed the brakes and we skidded to a stop right at their feet.

'Hey, Moone,' grunted Conor Bonner.

'Nice bike,' smirked Jonner Bonner.

They shared a look and I suddenly had a sinking feeling. 'Aw, balls,' I moaned.

'Can I 'ave a go on it?' asked Jonner Bonner, who was already climbing on, pushing Martin off the seat.

'Er. Sure!' Martin smiled nervously.

Jonner cycled around on the bike. 'Nice. Very nice.'

'Oh. Thanks, Jonner Bonner.'

'Except for the buckle.'

'Buckle?' asked a worried Martin.

Jonner Bonner nodded. 'Front wheel's all buckled.'

'The back one looks a bit wonky too,' added his brother. 'Want us to straighten them out for you, Moone?'

'Er . . .'

And before Martin could say anything more, the brothers had dumped the bike on the ground and were jumping up and down on it like they were testing out a new trampoline.

Our mouths dropped in horror.

'Woah!' I cried. 'That's not how you fix a buckle! Is it . . . ?'

'T-take it easy there, lads,' Martin squeaked meekly.

But the brothers ignored him.

I'd love to say that at this point we both charged forward and attacked them valiantly. But in truth, we just stood there. It was pretty feeble, I know, but what else could we do? One of us was a coward. And the other was a figment of the coward's imagination. We weren't much of a match for Boyle's psycho siblings.

Just then Padraic arrived behind us, panting and completely out of breath. He was covered in sweat, as if he'd been following us for miles.

Which of course he had.

'I said,' he wheezed at Martin, 'any chance I could . . . have a go on –'

He then noticed the Bonners leaping up and down on the bike, and stepped back. 'Oh. Never mind. It looked nicer earlier on.' And he hurried away as fast as his little legs could carry him.

A little later, Liam was holding the battered bike in the Moone kitchen, demanding answers.

'You cycled into a door?' he asked incredulously.

Martin nodded sadly. 'It just . . . came out of nowhere.'

'But it's wrecked, Martin. How many times did you cycle into the door?'

I leaned in to advise him, feeding him lines.

'There were two doors,' Martin explained to his dad.

'Which doors? Where?'

Debra came forward, bending down towards Martin. 'What really happened, Martin? This isn't the first time you've banged into things. Do you remember that time you said you fell into a tree? But that's not even possible, is it?'

'Well, to be honest, the bike fell apart pretty easily.'

'There were no structural problems with that bike, Martin Moone!' snapped Liam. He'd assembled the bike himself and only had five bolts and three nuts left over, which was a good result for Liam.

'Was it those Bonner boys again?' asked Debra, then turned to Liam. 'They've been giving him a hard time at school.'

Liam and Debra both looked at Martin, but he said nothing, lowering his sad little eyes. It was all the confirmation Liam needed. 'Right,' he said with a determined voice, and marched out of the room.

'Where are you going?' asked Debra.

Liam returned, pulling on his jacket. 'Nobody bullies my boy,' he told them. 'Except . . . maybe Sinead.'

Sinead looked up from her fourth bowl of Readybix and gave a nod in agreement.

'You gonna teach them a lesson they'll never forget, Dad?' asked Martin hopefully.

Liam stared into the middle distance and turned up his collar like a man on a mission. 'I'm going to go and speak to their father. If it's a pleasant chat, fine. If not, so be it.'

We couldn't believe it. Liam was going to take on the Bonners!

'That's what I'm talking about!' I said as I watched him stride away purposefully. Finally a Moone who meant business.

Debra looked at her bored daughters, slouched at the table, and at Martin, who was still staring down at his mangled heap of a bicycle.

'Well, nothing lifts the spirits like a nice bowl of Readybix,' she said kindly.

Martin and the girls all groaned.

## CHAPTER TWENTY-ONE
## A BULLY'S BULLY

That night, Martin gazed thoughtfully up at the stars. (He had those glow-in-the-dark stickers on the ceiling above his bed.) His spirit felt as battered and bruised as his new bike. What can we do about these flippin' bullies? he thought.

'Ya know, buddy, we could just leave the country? Steal a ship, kidnap a crew, navigate the violent Atlantic Ocean and make a new home in Padraic's South America,' I brilliantly suggested.

'Ah, that's just the easy way out!'

'Can't argue with that logic.'

'I'm sure Dad will sort it out – he looked quite determined earlier.'

'Was that what that look was? I just thought

he was constipated*. Ya know, I think you're
right, buddy. I mean . . . he could see how
disappointed you were. You're his only son. I bet
he's putting manners on those terrible twins
right now!'

'Knock knock knock,' Liam whispered, as
he entered Martin's bedroom very gingerly**
indeed. And he wasn't alone. He brought with
him into the room an almighty whiff of gin.

'Heeey, buddy, how ya doin'?' he half
burped.

'I'm OK, Dad. How are you?' asked the
worried boy.

Liam tiptoed slowly from the door and
finally flopped on to the edge of Martin's bed.
The gin aroma was pretty pungent by now.

'I'm good. How are you?' Liam repeated.

*CONSTIPATED – when poos get stuck in your
belly. This is usually caused by eating
candles.

**GINGERLY – another word for carefully.
As in, 'Ginger Jim gingerly chopped some
ginger for his gin.'

Determined to discover his fate, an unfazed Martin pushed ahead.

'So . . . how did the Bonner battering go, Dad?'

Liam seemed to have no idea what his last-born was talking about, until finally –'Oh yeahhh!!' he remembered, a little too loud. 'Listen . . . you should steer well clear of those Bonner boys. They sound awful.'

His answer gave me the impression that maybe Liam had not disciplined the Bonner boys at all. There's a fair chance he'd ended up going to the pub instead. Who knows? But a hopeful Martin still had faith in his delicately drunken dad.

'But, Dad . . .'

'All righty then, night-night, hairy head,' Liam slurred as he roughly ruffled his son's head with his heavy, hammered hand.

Martin hoped for some final words of comfort, but could only watch in dismay as Liam stood up with a little fart and wandered off, humming tipsily to himself.

As he observed his father navigate the tricky doorway, Martin turned to me, dejected.

'I feel like he didn't kill them.'

'Nope – I think you're gonna need to deal with this one yourself, buddy. Ya know what we need?'

We both considered what single solution could finally rid us of those wretched Bonner brothers. We sat in silence, thinking deep into our thought jellies for what seemed like a dozen seconds, until eventually we exclaimed together –

'A bully protector!' he said.

'A rabid dog!' said I. 'Or a bully protector!' I agreed, to keep things simple.

A bully protector. Perfect. Someone with the authority and machismo* to act as an anti-Bonner guardian. But who could handle that terribly tough task? It was quite the pickle.

*MACHISMO – a manly strength some men gain by drinking Italian coffee.

'Superman?!' Martin suggested.

'Might be tricky to get him on such short notice,' I replied.

'Spider-Man?'

'Same problem really, buddy.'

We thought on.

For quite a while.

'DECLAN MANNION!' we finally announced in unison.

Declan Mannion, the elder statesman in Martin's class, was an expert in the art of bullying. But not the dirty slaps and amateur rough-housing method the Bonner brothers practised. Declan was a bully's bully. Feared and respected in equal measure, he brought a degree of class and innovation to the whole bullying game.

He treated bullying like a small business. He'd take your lunch money every Monday and use that cash to bet on greyhound races. But if his hound won, he'd return your funds without interest every Friday. He'd keep the interest and gambling gains for himself. Like a teenage thug bank. And how did he squeeze your pennies from you? Well, brute force mostly. But even his methods of torture were original.

He was the master of the reverse wedgie. He could make a towel snap like a cowboy's whip. He even added an element of witchcraft to the Wet Willy manoeuvre.

But he was probably best known for his fresh take on the Chinese Burn. 'The Cambodian Burn' used a technique similar to the Chinese Burn, but on completion revealed Declan's name on his victim's forearm.

It was decided. Declan was our man.

The next morning at school, we spotted Mannion and his minions sitting on the steps of the old science building. He was reading the *Racing Past* and chewing tobacco.

'All right, Martin, this is your chance,' I said. 'You need to butter him up and get to business quickly so we can get on with our lives, Bonner-free. Don't be afraid, get over there. And use an authoritative but respectful tone.'

Martin nodded and approached Declan with purpose.

'Mr Mannion, may I have a word, sir?'

'What's troubling you, Moone-face?' Declan enquired, without ever lifting his head from his paper.

'Well . . . I'm having a little bother with the Bonner brothers . . .'

'And you're looking for protection, I suppose?' Declan said. He was clearly asked for this frequently, which was encouraging in a way.

'Well, yes, I thought maybe . . .'

'It's a service I provide, sure. Gonna cost ya though.'

And so the bargaining began. Martin estimated that he had 40p in his pocket. But if Declan wanted more than that, he'd happily sell all his schoolbooks and maybe some of his hair. This was important.

'Ehm, OK. Cost me what, roughly?'

Declan took his account book from his nearest minion and checked the going rate for bully protection.

'A feel of your sister's boobs,' he said casually.

*Gulp.*

'I'm sorry – what was that?'

'A feel of your sister's boobs,' Mannion repeated.

Martin was a little thrown by Declan's asking price, but tried to stay cool.

'Yeah, that's what I thought you sa—'

'Take it or leave it, Marty McCry,' Declan

interrupted, before sticking his nose back into his *Racing Past*.

Martin looked to me for guidance. Which was unwise. I'm a pretty poor guide at the best of times. And a terrible cub scout at the worst of times.

I shrugged. 'Seems fair to me.'

Martin turned back to his new colleague and offered a manly handshake. 'We have ourselves a deal, sir.'

'We'll detail it laters. Leave me now. These hounds won't pick 'emselves,' Declan said, without ever raising his nose from his canine form guide.

Martin nodded awkwardly and started to walk away, happy to have made progress.

'Wait, buddy,' I said. 'Don't you think you've forgotten something?'

Martin considered this and quickly caught my drift. He turned on his heel and approached Declan.

'Excuse me, Mr Mannion, just one more thing. Which sister?'

Mannion folded over his paper, clearly growing bored of Martin's interruptions.

'Whoever has the biggest boobs, ya tit.'

*Gulp.*

## CHAPTER TWENTY-TWO
## THE BOOBY TRAP

Martin had never paid much notice to his sisters' boobs before. Or anyone's boobs, to be honest. They'd always seemed like such cumbersome lumps. He had no interest in boobs, and swore he never would. But to save himself from further Bonner beatings, he needed to find out which sister had the misfortune of having the largest chest sacks. He knew they wore bras, and presumed that they must come in different dimensions. He figured that bra size would hold that precious information, as well as the owner's names, as was the case with all Moone underwear. So he headed into the back garden to study the washing line of weather-beaten boulder holders.

The bras had a selection of letters and
numbers on their tags: 32B, 28C, 34AA. Martin
presumed these were probably some kind of
maths puzzle. Struggling to work out which bra
was biggest, he tried each bra cup on his head,
to see if he could gauge their size as hats. This
worked a treat. On weighing up their assets,
it seemed to be Trisha who was best suited
for Declan's needs. As he removed his sister's
bra from his head, Martin was delighted that
for once he'd completed a tricky task without
embarrassing himself.

As he finished that happy thought, he heard a rattle on the kitchen window and turned in horror to find Fidelma, Trisha, Sinead and his mam staring angrily at him from inside. They'd obviously been watching his underwear experiment for quite a while and looked none too pleased. He'd been caught bra-handed. And bra-headed.

'Quick!' I said. 'Make yourself look busy, buddy.'

At that, Martin grabbed a nearby wheelbarrow. He forced an awkward smile and began rolling it purposefully past the kitchen window.

'Just picking some spring spuds,' he offered, as he strolled by the glaring gals.

It wasn't springtime. And the Moones didn't grow potatoes. But he was pretty sure the ladies weren't aware of these facts.

Before approaching Trisha with his request, we thought it best to cover our tracks. Martin found some potato-shaped rocks in the garden and covered them in muck. Then he tossed them in the wheelbarrow and rolled into the kitchen like a fresh-faced farmer. His mother shouted at him for making such a mess, but at least his spud story now looked true. Martin hated the idea of being thought of as a liar. Especially when he *was* lying. Which was often.

With his tracks now covered in spuds, he went about convincing Trisha to go on a date with Declan Mannion. He needed to butter her up. An amazing gift to lighten her spirits should do it.

'Flowers?' I suggested.

'Ah, I've been in the garden all flippin' morning,' Martin replied.

'Chocolates? Diamonds?'

'No, gotta be something that packs a punch, CustServRep263. A gift that keeps on giving. After all, I'm asking her to offer a boob squeeze to a stranger.'

We thought longish and hardish for what seemed like nearly no time at all.

'A cup of tea!' we said in unison. The perfect bribe. Our best ideas were always the ones we came up with together. It was actually surprising we didn't say more things at the same time, considering I'm just a figment of Martin's imagination.

'Hey, Trish . . .' Martin smiled as he entered his sister's bedroom. 'Made you a nice cuppa tea.'

He awaited her huge, thankful response. But she just looked confused as she took the mug from his grasp and tasted it.

'It's cold,' she barked.

'Ohhh. Are you a *hot* tea drinker? I'm sorry, I wasn't aware.'

Fidelma, who was lying on the other bed listening to music and reading *Countrypolitan**, looked up and shook her head. This wasn't encouraging.

*COUNTRYPOLITAN – a magazine for rural young ladies. It specializes in articles like 'How to Find the Perfect Clover' and 'Six Ways to Please Your Mam'.

'Anyhoo . . .' Martin continued hopefully, 'I was wondering if you might do me a wee favour . . .'

'Probably not. What do you want?' Trisha grunted, sipping her cold tea.

'Well . . . Silly thing really . . . Ya know the way you have boobs . . . ?'

There was a marked silence as Trisha and Fidelma stared at their little brother in shock.

'Excuse me?' Trisha said.

'Boobs,' Martin repeated. 'Those things.' He pointed at her chest, hoping to ease any confusion.

Fidelma now got involved. 'Excuse me?!' she shrieked, pulling off her headphones.

'Boobs, Fidelma, boobs. Lady hills. Blubber bags. Boobies. You have them too. But yours are smaller so they're of no use to me.'

'What are you on about, ya twerp?!' Trisha snapped.

'Well . . .' Martin started, 'I won't bore you with the whole drama, but let's just say there's

246

an acquaintance* of mine at school who has promised me a favour for a fondle of one of your boobies. It's really that simple.'

The girls looked aghast. I don't know why. Maybe it still wasn't simple enough. They weren't the brightest.

'WHO?!' Trisha snarled.

'Well, I'm not sure you know him. The gentleman's name is Declan Mannion—'

'Bring me to him! NOW!'

'Wow, I didn't think it would be this easy, buddy,' I whispered, as we watched Trisha stand up, grab a baseball bat from under her bed and charge to the door.

We found Declan and his minions sitting on a bench in the 'pleasure grounds**' by the old

---

*ACQUAINTANCE - someone you only kinda know. And you'll probably forget later in life. A stranger you haven't yet made.

**PLEASURE GROUNDS - a playground where older teenagers in Boyle go to practise French-kissing***.

***FRENCH KISSING - the process where a girl tries to remove any frog's legs a boy has got caught between his teeth using only her tongue.

Boyle river. It was called the old river because, like an old person, it moved quite slowly and often lost its way. This caused schools and hospitals to get flooded every winter.

Once she spotted him, Trisha marched towards Declan with the ferocity and violence of a lady in love. Then the shouting started.

'Wait a second, buddy, I think she's angry with him.'

'I believe she is,' Martin agreed. 'We really should have seen that coming.'

The shouting soon turned to screaming. To his credit, Declan just sat there patiently, taking the barrage of abuse like a champ. Then the screaming turned to cursing. I can't write much of what Trisha said then, as I've never used such terrible words, so I don't know how to spell them. But it was becoming clear that any interest Declan had in Martin's sister's anatomy was surely disappearing with every ugly insult.

'The plan isn't going brilliantly,' Martin admitted as we watched Trisha call Declan every name in the Moone cursing dictionary.

I felt bad that Martin had to witness such

shocking language,
so I grabbed a nearby
banjo and drowned
out Trisha's wicked
words. It was standard
IF behaviour. My sweet
stringed tune played loudly
as Trisha hurled her anger
over Declan's startled face.

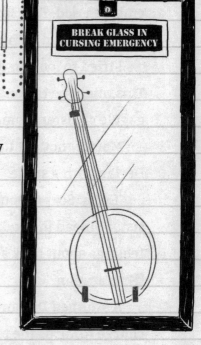

'The only part of my
body you'll ever feel is
my foot kicking ya up the
arse. You . . . You . . .' She
stopped to take a breath.
Her rage seemed to be getting a little sleepy.

'I think she's done,' Martin hoped. 'Looks like
she can't—'

'Got that? Ya filthy little nud?!' Trisha
snarled, before finally kicking Declan in the
shins and storming off.

Martin and I shared a look of concern as we walked towards a truly shell-shocked Mannion.

He'd been ridiculed, snarled at and embarrassed. This surely spelled the end of any interest he had in Trisha's affections.

I tried to look on the bright side. 'Hey, buddy. This might be the one time where having a gaggle of sisters comes in useful.'

Martin thought this over and approached Declan with a smile.

'Haha. Sorry about that. Let's talk about my sister Sinead instead. What are your general feelings about back acne . . . ?' No answer came. 'Mr Mannion?'

A stunned Declan was still watching Trisha charge towards the pleasure-grounds exit, tipping over garbage bins and schoolboys as she went.

'I think I'm in love,' he mumbled.

# CHAPTER TWENTY-THREE
## POETRY IN SLOW MOTION

With Declan's heart set on Trisha, maybe all was not lost. But how could we convince her to go on a date with Mannion after she'd verbally bashed him so brutally? What could turn such a girl's head in this crazy, lazy world? It was time to go shopping.

We met Declan at BetterBuys.

'Would she like that?' Declan said, as he held up a toy bear. We'd been browsing the aisles for quite a while and it was becoming clear that Declan was not used to buying 'girl gifts'. Prior to the teddy bear, he'd suggested we bribe Trisha with a toilet seat, a tub of butter, a garden hose and a packet of those furry things you put on the bottom of chair legs to stop them scraping floors.

'Ahmm . . .' Martin pondered as he considered the sad-looking teddy, 'I'm not sure she's really into . . . soft things—'

'This?' quizzed Mannion, now holding aloft a cheap plastic paper-stapler.

Martin's mind briefly wandered to a memory he had of Trisha stapling his sleeve to the kitchen table once after he'd stolen one of her chips at dinner.

'I think she's OK for staplers, Decla—'

'That?' interrupted Mannion once more.

This time he was proudly holding up a tin of chicken-flavour soup*. Although on the front it said, 'Chicken-flava,' maybe to make it sound funky.

'Soup?' asked Martin, unsure.

Declan snorted. 'Everyone likes soup.'

'Ahmm . . . Yeah, I suppose they—'

*CHICKEN-FLAVOUR SOUP – this soup, like all chicken-flavoured canned goods, is guaranteed to contain zero actual chicken. Ideal for chicken-haters.

'Great, give me your money, I don't have any money.'

Martin sadly dug his last pennies from his shallow pockets and handed them over. And off Declan went to the counter, stupidly satisfied with his seductive soup.

But Martin suspected that a little more than fowl-flava soup might be required to win Trisha's heart. Romance. That's what we needed. Chicken-flava romance.

Back in his bedroom, Martin and I set about writing a poem to serve with the soup. Poems are the most romantic thing you can do. Poetry first began when Adam tried to tempt Eve away from the evil serpent in the Garden of Eden. She couldn't decide between marriage and fruit. So Adam said:

> *I promise we'll marry when I find a*
> *  decent chapel,*
> *So forget about that snake with his*
> *  rotten-lookin' apple.*

That's why the cheeky snake chose to tempt Eve with an apple. Nothing rhymes with orange.

Anyway . . . if it was good enough for the first couple, it'd be good enough for Trisha. We decided Declan was probably not a poetry nut, so we set about composing a romantic sonnet* ourselves.

'*Dear Trisha Moone,*' Martin started informatively, '*You seem pretty mad. That makes me sad. Which is bad.*'

'Solid opening, buddy,' I encouraged him. 'But maybe it could sound a little more . . . exciting? We need to catch her attention. Our words need to be like a big romantic volcano!'

'Got it!' Martin said, as he licked the end of his pencil with excitement. He then swallowed the horrible taste of pencil lead and hit his poetry page with some big stupid love words.

*SONNET – a kind of poem where you only rhyme every now and again. Perfect for when you forget you're supposed to be writing a poem.

'*Your fire burns bright. Like the sun. Which is incredibly hot. Like a fire. Which burns bright, like . . . the sun!*'

'That's it, buddy. That's it! You'll seduce your sister yet!'

'I flippin' hope so, CustServRep263.'

'So what other treats can we expect in your volcanic verse?' I asked.

'Should I mention something about how Trisha burns everything she cooks?'

'Hard to make that sound romantic. Maybe write something nice about her looks?'

'Good thinking, beard-face! How about this? *I love your . . . mousy hair. Like a beautiful . . . mouse. And your pale, blemished\* skin. And your scent. You smell even nicer than . . .*'

We stopped to think of the most glorious aroma we could imagine.

'Crisps?' I offered.

'Perfecto! *Crisps*.' Martin wrote it down.

*BLEMISHED - spot-ridden.

'*Regards, Mr Mannion.*' He signed off with a flourish.

'What a poem!' I said as I gave Martin a well-deserved high five. 'If that doesn't work, I really don't understand women at all.'

'I smell like *crisps*?!' The tone in Trisha's voice suggested that she wasn't as impressed by smoky bacon or cheese and onion as we were.

'*Nicer* than crisps,' corrected Martin. 'It's a compliment.'

She got up from her bed and read over the poem very carefully. She didn't seem to be falling for our romantic gesture at all.

'Blemished skin?!' she snarled.

'Quick, Martin, break out the big guns,' I whispered.

'Oh, he got you this as well.' Martin handed her the tin of chicken-flava soup.

'Soup?!' she asked.

'The thinking man's tea!' Martin assured her. He'd heard that on an advert on the telly, for a product he couldn't remember. Probably soup.

Trisha studied the poem once more, then looked back at the tin of 'fowl' broth. She suddenly seemed a little worried and asked quietly, 'Is Declan in the . . . "special class"?'

'If by special, you mean *cool*, then, YES! He's the coolest kid in school – that's probably why they won't let him leave.'

Her ears pricked up when she heard the word 'cool'. Coolness was very important to Trisha. Martin never knew why. His other sister, Fidelma, was always trying to look 'hot'. But Trisha always wanted to look cool. Women seemed to be divided by temperature. Martin had always loved being 'luke-warm'. He was a tepid nut.

'Oh, wait – is this all like . . . taking the piss out of love letters and stuff?' Trisha asked, suddenly interested. 'Like . . . in an ironic way?'

'Ahmm . . . Yeah! Obviously,' Martin lied. He wasn't actually sure what ironic meant.

'Huh. That's kinda *funny*. I guess.' Trisha looked back at the poem in a fresh light. She even giggled a little. Which was a disturbing sound.

'So . . . ya think maybe you'd like to meet up with Declan again? And maybe not shout at him so much this time?' Martin asked.

Trisha looked at the poem and pulled her coolest face. 'Whatever.' She shrugged, and went off, laughing at the soup like a weirdo.

## CHAPTER TWENTY-FOUR
## THE SHIFT

The next day, Trisha and Declan Mannion were
standing together on the edge of the lake,
cooing at each other like a couple of lovebirds.
Well, maybe not 'cooing' as such. It was more
of a long awkward silence really. And with
their black coats and threatening faces, these
'lovebirds' probably looked more like a couple
of surly crows. But they were at the lake at
least – the most romantic spot in all of Boyle,
Right Beside Boyle and Just Outside Boyle.
Trisha loved feeding the ducks. She always had.
Ever since she was a little girl. And a girl never
changes the things she likes doing. That's a
well-known fact. I think.

It was their first date, and we'd imagined
them basking in the sunshine at the water's

259

edge, maybe having an impromptu* picnic, as Declan whispered sweet poetry into her ear. But it turned out to be a cold, grey, blustery day and Martin had forgotten to bring the picnic. We'd also forgotten to write a new poem. But if anyone could come up with some sappy spiel** on the spot, then surely it was Declan Mannion.

*IMPROMPTU – unplanned. Short for IMpossibly PRobable Obviously Made-Up Plot TUrns. Like a hastily written novel.

**SPIEL – a sack of nonsense spun by a silver-tongued scamp.

Or so we'd hoped.

They stood in total silence for several long minutes before Declan finally spoke. 'Well . . . this is pleasant.'

Trisha eyed him warily, then looked back at the water again.

More silence.

Martin and I were watching from behind a tree and were getting more anxious by the moment.

'What did he say?' Martin whispered to me.

'I think he said, "Well . . . this is pleasant."'

'*Pleasant*?! What?! Does he think he's at a flippin' flower fair?' asked Martin, perplexed. 'The man can drive a bus, for God's sake! Surely he can woo a woman!'

'I don't know, buddy. He's looking pretty useless out there. Maybe we've discovered Declan Mannion's kryptonite*.

*KRYPTONITE - the green crystals that make Superman powerless. But if you don't have any kryptonite to hand, a dodgy Indian curry will have exactly the same effect on him, and for a fraction of the price.

261

His one weakness. Maybe romancing a lady is the one thing he *can't* do.'

'Don't even say that! If this doesn't go well, then we've lost our bully's bully. And without a bully's bully, we're bully fodder!'

I could see Trisha fidgeting, glancing towards the exit of the park.

'She's getting restless,' I whispered. 'I think she's gonna walk.'

'No!' squealed Martin in a panic.

His sister didn't notice the squeal from the tree behind her – thankfully her hearing had been permanently damaged during a Pogues* concert the previous summer – but Declan looked back.

Martin made an urgent gesture to feed the ducks. He had provided Declan with a bag of breadcrumbs for just this purpose, but Declan seemed to have forgotten all about it.

*THE POGUES – a shower of mad music-makers led by a toothless genius.

He gave a nod to Martin and opened up the bag, which was damp from his sweaty palms.

'Here, ducks!' he shouted loudly, and flung a fistful of crumbled loaf.

A family of ducks flapped and splashed their way over.

'You're feeding the ducks?' asked Trisha, with raised eyebrows, as if this was the most un-cool thing she'd ever witnessed.

'Er yeah,' replied Declan. 'Martin said you like feeding them.'

'When I was about ten. I don't feed the ducks any more.'

Declan grimaced uncomfortably and crumpled up the bag. 'Of course not. Flip off, ducks!' he yelled.

The startled ducks flew off, and the lake returned to silence.

We continued to watch, but I could barely bear this awkwardness any more. 'What's he waiting for?' I demanded impatiently. 'Go on, man, lunge! Lunge!'

Trisha gestured towards home. 'Well, I should probably be heading ba—'

Suddenly Declan pounced. He lurched forward, planting his lips firmly on Trisha's. She seemed a little surprised, but didn't object. Mannion kissed her passionately. Firmly but gently. Tenderly but vigorously. Smoothly but damply.

Martin grinned with glee, rubbing his hands together. 'That's it. Kiss her. Kiss her good. Shift my sister.'

This concerned me a little. But I decided not to dwell on it.

Finally Declan unstuck his lips from Trisha with a *shlurrpp* and gave a nod of approval.

'Deadly.' He smiled, and then strutted happily away.

Trisha shrugged indifferently and strolled off in the opposite direction.

'Yes!' cried Martin triumphantly. 'We're one step closer to having a bully protector! All the pieces of the jigsaw are finally coming together!'

'They sure are,' I nodded, not quite as confidently. 'Although . . . it really is an odd sort of jigsaw, isn't it? Maybe we should just play cards instead.'

Just then, a tubby, upside-down clown swung into view, giving us both a hop.

'BOO!'

'Lou!'

'Cuckoo!' beamed the bumbling buffoon. His legs were wrapped around a branch and he was hanging down from the tree above us, like an obese monkey.

'What is it with you and flippin' foliage*?' I demanded, irritated. 'Do you have to keep leaping out of leaves?'

'A *real* imaginary knows how to make an entrance, hairball!' He smirked smugly. 'But I guess they don't teach that in Customer Service School! Hahaha!'

He cackled with laughter and then tried to

*FOLIAGE – a fancy word for leaves that comes from the word 'foal', meaning a young horse. This is because, long ago, young trees and bushes were less lazy than today and would often canter and gallop around the countryside.

266

swing himself coolly out of the tree, but it didn't go quite right and he landed face first in a heap on the ground.

'Whoopsie!' he sang, pretending it didn't hurt.

He then clambered awkwardly to his feet, dusted himself off and smiled broadly at us both. 'What ya up to, fellas? Saying your final farewells?'

Martin frowned at him. 'Why would we be doing that?'

'Oh, I don't know,' he answered coyly. 'Just in case something happened to your new pal here. It'd be a real shame if he just suddenly . . . went away . . . forever!'

'Went away forever where?' I asked. 'I'm not going anywhere!'

'Maybe not.' Lou shrugged. 'But sometimes things just disappear. Like this flower here.'

He held a little daisy and tried to do a trick to make it magically disappear. But it didn't quite work and the daisy fell to the ground.

'What are you on about, Lou?' asked Martin, getting annoyed.

'Oh, nothing, Moo-Moo. All I'm saying is that it'd be an awful shame if this big galloo happened to get hisself evicted.'

'Evicted?!' I exclaimed.

'What do you mean, evicted?' demanded Martin. 'Evicted from where?'

'From your imagination, Marty Moo. After all, he ain't supposed to be there. Loopy Lou was here first.'

Martin looked at me, a little worried. 'Is that a thing?' he asked me. 'Can you be . . . evicted?'

I have to admit, I was wondering the same thing. I had a vague memory of imaginary evictions being explained to us in Customer Service training, but that day I think I might have been more focused on hitting Boring Brenda on the head with a paper aeroplane.

I gave Martin a reassuring smile. 'Don't worry, buddy. No one's evicting me.'

But Lou smirked at us smugly. 'I just hope

that's all they do to you, sneaky-poo. The C.L.I.F.F. Council tend to frowny-frown on realsie-robbing.'

'Realsie-robbing?!' I laughed. 'Martin *chose* me, Lou! So just get over it, will ya? You're hanging around like a bad smell. Who smells bad.'

Lou advanced closer, looking menacing – or as menacing as anyone can look while wearing polka-dot trousers and one large clown shoe. 'I'll get over it as soon as *you* get outta here. Back to surveys and pencil-pushing! Back to where you belong!'

'Oh yeah? And who's gonna make me?'

'Me, that's who! *I'm* the ducks now, tall-head! *I'm* the ducks!' he repeated, like a maniac.

'Guys, guys, guys, please!' called Martin, pushing his way between us. 'I know you both want to be my IF. And to be honest – who can blame you? I'm an excellent realsie. But there's plenty of Martin Moone to go around. Can't we all just get along?'

There was a pause as Lou and I glared at each other.

But then suddenly I had an idea, and I smiled deviously. 'You know what? The little idiot is right. Enough of this silly squabbling. Let's have some fun!'

'That's more like it.' Martin smiled. 'What'll we do?'

'Well, we're right beside Boyle Forest,' I said, gesturing at the line of trees behind us. 'How about we all go and play a nice game of hide-and-seek?'

'Now you're talkin'! Just the thing to help us

unwind after watching all that intense shifting. Lou, are you in?'

Lou hesitated and glanced at me, unsure. But I knew he wouldn't be able to resist. 'Of course I'm in, Marty Moo!' he smiled. 'I'm a hide-and-seek freakanatic!'

And so Martin and I strode off towards the forest with Loopy Lou skipping and whistling behind us. But little did that bumbling oaf know, I had a plan to get rid of him once and for all.

## CHAPTER TWENTY-FIVE
## A QUARREL WITH LAUREL

'We've been walking for ages, CustServRep263!'
complained Martin. 'Can't we just play hide-
and-seek here?'

I came to a stop and looked around. I'd led
Martin and Lou deep into the forest, to the
darkest, most tangly part of it. It was the perfect
place for someone to get lost. *Permanently* lost!

'Yes, this'll do nicely,' I said with a devilish
glint in my eye, and then cackled like an evil
genius. 'MWAHAHAHAHAHA!'

But I stopped when I saw Martin and Lou
looking at me. 'Oh, er, sorry. Didn't mean to do
that out loud.'

'No problemo!' said Martin pleasantly.
'We're all very excited about this game of
hide-and-seek.'

'Then let's get hiding!' I said. 'And Lou, you do the seeking!'

'Don't mind if I do!' he beamed excitedly.

'Give us a good head start,' I told him. 'Count to five thousand!'

'Five thousand?! Sounds like we're playing Hide-And-Seek-ULTRA! My favourite!'

He covered his eyes enthusiastically and started counting. 'One Mississippi! Two Mississippi! Three Mississippi*!'

I grabbed Martin and led him away through the trees. 'Quick, buddy, let's ditch that dope. He'll never find his way back from here. And he can take his eviction and shove it!'

Martin looked at me. 'I thought you weren't worried about that.'

'Oh. Er, I'm not. It's just . . .'

'Just what?'

*ONE MISSISSIPPI – a phrase used to count out a second. Unless you say it too quickly. Fast-talkers need to say, 'One Missy-Misses-Mississippi, Two Missy-Misses-Mississippi,' and so on. Good luck with that.

'Well . . .' I looked down as we walked.
'. . . The thing is, when Lou says that I'm not a proper imaginary friend . . . he does sort of have a point,' I admitted.

'How do you mean?'

'Well, I don't have a licence, I've never been schooled in the Art of Imaginary Friendship. I've never taken the Oath. I've never held the Sacred Spoon* or bonged the Great Gong. I've never worn the Enchanted Duffle Coat or sipped from the Ancient Goblet of IFfyness. My middle toes haven't been removed, and I don't have a secret tattoo on my left bum cheek—'

'Wow, becoming an imaginary friend is really involved, isn't it?'

'It's *incredibly* involved! And I've done none of it! I don't even have any funny clothes.'

'Your suits always look a bit tight on the shoulders . . .' Martin offered kindly.

*SACRED SPOON – a magical soup spoon that's completely dripless. Legend has it that even a man with shaky hands can eat a bowl of tomato soup with it while wearing a white shirt, and still remain miraculously splatter-free.

'Aw, thanks, buddy.' I smiled. 'But the fact is, Loopy Lou is more qualified. He outranks me. I'm just a middle man, Martin. I do surveys. I file reports. The most exciting thing I ever do in my job is make pie charts.'

'Those sound tasty!'

'Well, that's what you might think, but they're not! They're just flippin' graphs! I can't go back to that life, buddy. I just can't! I can't spend my days doing paperwork again, squashed in a cubicle and munching on pie charts!'

'Oh, CustServRep263, stop worrying your silly little head,' Martin reassured me. 'You're my imaginary friend! You're not going anywhere.' He gave me a comforting smile. 'But if you're worried about Lou, then let's just lose that looper properly once and for all.'

I high-fived him happily and we sprinted off through the trees.

Twenty minutes later we were completely lost. We seemed to be going around in circles and the whole 'losing Lou' thing wasn't quite going to plan as we kept accidentally finding him again. He was still counting away when we stumbled upon him for the third time.

'Two thousand and sixteen Mississippi! Two thousand and seventeen Mississippi!'

'That's it, Lou, keep counting!' I called, as we ran off once more. Well, I ran, Martin turned and crashed straight into a tree.

He held his battered nose and looked up at the massive trunk.

'Who put this stupid flippin' tree here . . .
oh! Sorry, Bruce! Took a rubbin' to me noggin
there,' Martin apologized. He then turned to a
shrub, 'Nice to see you again too, Laurel,' and
gave its branches a warm handshake.

'No dis jus mulberry bush, stoopid!' snapped
Bruce. 'Where Laurel? Laurel!!'

A laurel bush cantered over to us, a little out
of breath. 'Ah, you found them, Bruce. Fair play,
boy.'

Martin waved. 'Hi, Laurel!' But Laurel turned
to me instead, looking rather stern.

'Customer Service Representative 263749?'
he asked.

'That's . . . me,' I replied nervously.

He whipped out an official-looking
document and thrust it into my hand.

'You've been served, boyo.'

'What?' I frowned. 'Served what? I didn't
order anything! I'm not even hungry. Five
bees have flown in my mouth since we hit
the forest!'

'That's your Eviction Notice. You've got forty-eight hours to vacate this lad's imagination. Otherwise you'll be removed by force, boyo.'

# EVICTION NOTICE

We hereby declare that Customer Service Representative 263749 has been illegally residing in Martin Moone's imagination and practising imaginary friendship without a licence.

He must vacate Martin Moone's thoughts within **two days**, so that Mr Moone's rightful IF, Loopy Loopington Lou, can resume his post.

BY ORDER of the Corporate League of Imaginary Friends Federation

'Eviction Notice?!' I cried.

'Oh balls,' moaned Martin.

'You brought this on yourself, beardy-boy,'

scolded Laurel. 'You've been acting like a total langer*. Loopy Lou was here first. You were only supposed to do a survey – not take his job, like a big jammy dodger.'

'I *gave* him the job!' Martin interjected. 'I *want* him to be my imaginary friend!'

'But he's just a clerk! He hasn't even bonged the Gong, for Pete's sake. You can't replace an imaginary friend with an imaginary clerk!' said Laurel, turning to leave.

'Wait!' called Martin. 'We're sorry.'

The trees paused and Martin looked to Bruce, pleadingly. 'Please help us out here, will ya? How can we get CustServRep263 licensed? How can we make him a proper imaginary friend?'

Bruce paused for a moment, then scratched his trunk pensively. 'Well . . . dis is a funny one. And I don't means funny haha. I means funny hmmm. Realsies don't usually choose

---

*LANGER – an insult used by Cork people. It stands for 'Little Danger'. Like a blunt thumb tack. Or a wet fire.

unqualified riff-raffs to be their IFs.'

I was about to retort, but Martin gave me a little kick to shut me up.

'Ow!'

'Let's consultify de manual,' declared Bruce. He then reached inside one of his hollows and produced an enormous, ancient book called *The Big Massive Manual*. He put on his reading glasses and flicked through the pages until he found what he was looking for. 'Ah! Here we goes!' he said as he read through the passage.

'OK, bashically . . . de manual says that if an unlicensed IF who's chosen by a realsie can prove hishelf to be a worthy imaginary friend, then the C.L.I.F.F. can say yesh to upgrade him.'

'That's it?' I smiled, relieved. 'I'm totally worthy!'

'Big time!' agreed Martin. 'Solved! Eviction averted!'

'Ha!' laughed Laurel. 'Lads, even if that happened, he'd never be an IF in two days.

Too much paperwork. Too much Gong bonging.
You've got the ceremony, the Oath, the toe
removals, the tattoo . . .'

'He's right.' Bruce nodded. 'Laurel is from
Cork, but he no stoopid.'

'So how can we stop the eviction?' demanded
Martin.

'Very simples,' Bruce told him. 'All you do is
jus find anover home for da Loopy Lou.'

'Like . . . a new hedge?' I asked.

'No, no.' Bruce shook his head. '*Real* home!
In a real realsie! You need to find person who
don't have no imaginary friend – but wants one,
yesh? You shee now?'

'Not really,' replied Martin.

'You need to find a realsie with a vacant
imagination. Someone with spare room inshide
their head. Someone who wants to fill that
room with da Loopy Lou. And if they imagines
him just right, then Lou makes da leap.'

Martin and I looked at each other,
completely flummoxed.

Laurel the Laurel gave a laugh. 'Haha! Good luck with that, ye tree-racist langers!'

Bruce chuckled too. 'Haha. Yes, Laurel ish correct – you will almost certainly fail.' He then smiled broadly and clapped his twiggy hands together as we walked away, further into the woods.

I could tell Martin was worried by this new development. I too was more than a little concerned that the stress of all this might make him want to ditch me.

'Ya know, I've been thinking, CustServRep263,' Martin said.

'That never ends well,' I remarked.

'I've been thinking –' Martin rolled up the Eviction Notice and stuck it in his pocket – 'in all the confusion over your identity, I really should give you a proper name.'

'You don't like my name?'

'Well . . . it's got numbers in it. Which is kinda weird.'

'Fair point,' I said.

'I want you to have a name that sets you apart from everyone else in Ireland. Something unique. Something that stands out.'

'All right. Got any ideas?'

'I sure do,' he said.

'How about Trent "Powerboat" Beardiful?' I suggested.

'No,' Martin said, shaking his head.

'Max "Silverfingers" Talliforth?'

'Still not imaginative enough.'

'OK, so what do you have in mind?'

'Well, I've put my imagination into overdrive and I've come up with a name that nobody will ever forget!' Martin smiled.

'Brilliant! What's my new name?'

'Sean Murphy,' he said. Then waited for applause.

I stood in silence to let that settle.

'Isn't that the most common name in Ireland?'

'Because it's great!' Martin said.

'Right. OK, well . . . Maybe we can make it a

bit more exciting with a funky middle name,'
I said hopefully.

'I've got that sorted too.' Martin smiled.
'CAUTION!'

'Caution?' I asked.

'Caution,' he repeated. 'As in . . . careful who
you're messing with, fool. Caution!'

'So my new name is Sean "Caution" Murphy?

'That's right. What d'ya think?'

I turned it over in my head. It's not often you
get a new name.

'I love it!' I said.

'You do? Why?' Martin asked, thinking it was
a trick.

'I love it, because you gave it to me.' I smiled.

Then we high-fived and got lost together.

# CHAPTER TWENTY-SIX
## EVICTION SHMICTION

After our confab* with the conifers**, we eventually found our way out of the forest. We stood on the edge of the lake and mulled over what to do.

In the distance, we could still hear Loopy Lou counting away at the top of his voice. 'Four thousand and three Mississippi! Four thousand and four Mississippi!'

I unfurled the Eviction Notice and stared at it. 'Two days . . . That only gives us till Monday.'

'So this is our last weekend together?'

**\*CONFAB** – sounds like it means 'fabulous conversation', but it actually just means 'conversation'. The word for 'fabulous conversation' is actually ***fabconfab***.

**\*\*CONIFER** – an evergreen tree that grows cones. These cones are later sculpted as vessels for your ice cream.

asked Martin. He was looking at me with quite a worried expression. Or else he needed to do a wee. Both expressions were quite similar.

'Martin, I can see that you're worried – and/or you need to do a wee.'

'You're right on both counts, Sean Murphy.'

'Well, worry not, buddy. And wee not. Not yet. We can beat this!'

Martin nodded, perking up. 'You're so right! Why should we be slaves to our bloomin' bladders?'

'I mean, beat the eviction thing.'

'That makes more sense.' He nodded again. 'And it means we have an actual chance of success.'

'Of course we've got a chance, buddy! All we've got to do is find a new realsie for Loopy Lou. How hard can that be?'

'Yeah, there must be loads of people who want imaginary friends.'

'There's got to be billions! Let's brainstorm a list. Got your copybook?'

Martin whipped it out from his back pocket and we started a list of potential Lou adopters.

'Padraic?' he suggested.

'Already taken.'

'Mam?'

'I'm not sure your mother wants another hyperactive clown in the house.'

'Sinead?'

'Loopy Lou would be dust in a week.'

'True,' nodded Martin sadly.

List of Realsies To Take Over The Imagining of Loopy Lou

1. ~~Padraic~~
2. ~~Mam~~
3. ~~Sinead~~
4. ~~Dad~~
5. ~~Fidelma~~
6. Mr. ~~Jackson~~
7. ~~Postman Matt~~
8. The ~~Readybix~~ Kid
9. ~~Bruce The Spruce~~
10. ~~Loopy Lou~~
11.

I paced around, stroking my lovely beard pensively as we brainstormed. Beards are great for this sort of thing. In fact, this was the reason I'd grown one in the first place. But with all the pensive beard stroking, I couldn't really focus on much else. So our brainstorm didn't stay stormy for long and soon died down to a light brain-breeze. We were out of ideas.

'All right, we'll come back to this,' I told him. 'But don't worry, we'll think of something. No one's kicking me out, buddy. Eviction shmiction!'

And with that defiant rhyme, I ripped the Eviction Notice into shreds and hurled the pieces into the lake. Or at least, I tried to hurl them into the lake, but the little bits of paper just blew back into our faces.

'That's the spirit, Sean!' cheered Martin, as he picked a piece of Eviction Notice from his mouth.

'And in the meantime,' I told him, 'we'll press on with Operation Bully's Bully to deal with the Bonners.'

Martin nodded, looking worried again.
Even the very mention of the Bonner brothers
seemed to upset him.

'Don't worry about those thugs, Martin,' I
told him. 'As soon as we've got Declan Mannion
on our side . . .'

Martin was now hopping with worry from
one foot to the other.

'Wait, you just need to do a wee.'

'I really do,' he said, bolting for the bushes,
'But that doesn't mean I'm not worried!'

Stage One of Operation Bully's Bully was now
complete, and Martin had happily ticked it off
our list, but there was still a lot more to do . . .

OPERATION Bully's Bully

STAGE 1: ~~Declan and Trisha have a big shift at the lake.~~
STAGE 2: Declan and Trisha go on a date and he feels her boobs.
STAGE 3: Declan Mannion becomes my bully protector.
STAGE 4: Declan Mannion gives the Bonner Brothers wedgies.
STAGE 5: I sit back and enjoy life with a Twix.

We really were making a lot of lists these days. But I guess that's what happens when you're doing stuff. You need to be organized. And to be organized you need to make lists. Which, ironically, takes up a lot of time and stops you doing the stuff you're supposed to be doing. But without the lists, you can't remember the stuff you're supposed to be doing that you're not doing because you're making lists to make sure that the stuff you're supposed to be doing gets done. It's a vicious bicycle.

Once we got home, Martin poked his head into his sisters' room and found Trisha lounging on her bed, reading a magazine.

'Sooooooo . . . how did it go, little one?' asked Martin sweetly, as if he knew nothing at all about her swapping spit with Declan Mannion at the lake.

Trisha lowered her copy of *Rogue** magazine.

*ROGUE* - a fashion magazine dedicated to lady motorcyclists.

'He kisses like a washing machine,' she said bluntly.

Martin glanced at me – neither of us had any idea what this meant. But it sounded pretty impressive to us!

'A washing machine? Wow! He's so amazing, isn't he?' Martin marvelled, shaking his head with wonder.

Trisha rolled her eyes and returned to her magazine.

'How about a *proper* date tonight?' Martin suggested. 'To the pictures*? We'll pay.'

'*We?*' she asked with a frown.

'I mean, us . . . men. In this case, him. Declan.'

She lowered the magazine again, curious.

'What's on?'

Martin and I shared a look and smiled with

*THE PICTURES – an old term meaning the cinema, which is used by people in black-and-white movies and, for some reason, everyone in rural Ireland.

satisfaction. We had her now. The fish was hooked. All we had to do was reel her in. And get Declan Mannion to grope her scaly fish chest.

'I said, what's on, deaf-head?' she repeated loudly.

'Oh, right, sorry. *Edward Scissorhands\*.'*

She gave a grunt of approval and went back to her fashion mag.

Martin was pleased, and was clearly feeling a little overconfident, as he then came closer and sat down on her bed.

'Hey, Trish, I've been thinking. You know the way you've no friends? Who aren't weirdos. Could I interest you at all in a nice imaginary one?'

She looked up at him slowly.

*\*EDWARD SCISSORHANDS* – a film about a fella called Edward who has scissors for hands. He also has hairdryers for feet, but that doesn't seem to be an issue for some reason.

'Oh balls,' I murmured, just before she thumped him.

# CHAPTER TWENTY-SEVEN
## THE PLAN

An hour later we were back in Boyle's pleasure grounds where we'd found Declan Mannion reading the *Racing Past*. He was frowning at Martin.

'But if I wanted an imaginary friend, couldn't I just . . . imagine one?'

'Ha! Good luck with that,' chuckled Martin, shaking his head. 'Trust me – I'd be saving you a lot of trouble and a lot of stinging nettle stings. And he's as good as new, Declan. Barely used.'

'I don't know, Moone,' said Declan reluctantly. 'He's second-hand. Who knows where he's been?'

'Well, he's just been in my imagination.'

'And you think I'd want him in *my* imagination after he's been in *yours*?'

'Well, it's not like he's diseased or anything. And obviously I'd give him a good wash,' added Martin, trying to sweeten the deal.

Declan mulled it over, but then shook his head. 'Nah, I'm gonna pass.'

Martin nodded glumly and Declan tucked his newspaper into his jacket. 'So, back to the booby business. This film tonight – what's it about?'

'It's about a fella called Edward. With scissors for hands.'

'Like Freddy Krueger*?' asked Declan, intrigued.

'Yeah, I think it's a sequel,' lied Martin. 'So, listen. Once you've, *ya know* –' he gave a knowing wink – 'you'll keep your side of the bargain?'

'Fear not, Moone,' Declan assured him,

*FREDDY KRUEGER – the star of the horror-movie classic *A Nightmare on Elm Street*. Like Edward Scissorhands, he has sharp fingers, but Freddie does a lot less shrubbery-styling and a lot more disembowelling.

'Once a tit's been cupped, I can interrupt.'

Martin beamed happily. We were almost there.

'Oh, and keep kissing her like a washing machine. I think she likes that.'

'Sound*,' said Declan. 'I'll let you know the booby outcome anon. Stay tarty, Marty.'

He sauntered off and Martin waved goodbye. 'See ya later, Pal-igator!'

Declan shook his head as he went, disgusted by Martin's poor sign-off.

Martin glanced around. He was all alone now.

'A washing machine, huh?' he said to himself, intrigued.

He was curious about this shifting lark and wanted to know what it felt like. But since he couldn't actually shift his own face, he decided to try shifting his hand. So he held it up and

*SOUND – an Irish term for 'OK'. We used to say 'sshwwiggadingdonggg!' but shortened that sound to 'sound' as we're so busy nowadays.

began to kiss it passionately. He slobbered
over it, smooching it damply and softly, like a
washing machine on a 'delicates' cycle.

My FIRST LOVE

'Moone!' came a shout, and Martin looked up
from his hand-embrace, startled.

Once again, the Bonner brothers had proved
themselves rather skilled at finding Martin in
weird shifting situations.

'So you're shifting yourself now, Moone?'
smirked Jonner Bonner. 'Did you run out of
dead birds?'

They hopped off their bicycles and advanced
with menace, but Martin put up his hands
defiantly.

'Stop!' he shouted. And the brothers actually stopped, amused to hear him answering back for once.

'I'm too busy to get beaten up right now,' Martin told them. 'But ye can batter me tonight. Behind the cinema. Right after *Edward Scissorhands*!'

Conor Bonner gave an evil leer. 'It's a date, Moone.'

A worried Jonner Bonner added, 'But . . . not in a romantic way.'

The brothers nodded to each other and then headed off.

'Little do they know,' I chuckled, as we watched them go, 'that a certain Mr Mannion will have your back tonight, buddy.'

Martin grinned with excitement and high-fived the empty air beside him. At least, that's what it looked like to Padraic, who was ambling towards him, struggling to carry a fishing net and a big bag of sweets.

'Mmhey, Mmarrrhhtin!' he garbled

cheerfully. His cheeks were  jammed full of chocolate toffees, which made it difficult to speak and also made him look even more hamster-ish than usual.

'Hey, P-Diddly!' Martin smiled. 'Rockin' the hamster look, I see.'

'Mmn . . . Well, the ladies . . . (munch) . . . don't call me "sweet-cheeks" for nothin'.' He grinned, and then swallowed down the sweets with an almighty gulp – which seemed to cause him some pain. 'Urgh. Probably should've chewed those a bit more.'

Martin plucked a chocolate mouse from Padraic's paper bag and popped it in his mouth. 'What's with all the goodies? Having a midday feast?'

'Nah, just doing a little spot of fishin'.'

'Fishing?'

'Yup. Gonna see if I can catch one of those chocolate fish you were talking about before.'

Martin frowned slightly, glancing at the old

river that was drifting slowly past them. 'That feels like a long shot, P.'

'Well, Crunchie says you can catch anything so long as you've got the right bait!'

Padraic's imaginary friend, Crunchie Haystacks, nodded in agreement. 'You need chocolate to catch chocolate! That's simple science!'

'Well, it's definitely simple all right,' I murmured dubiously.

Just then, Padraic flung a fistful of choccies into the river.

'Woah! What are you doing?' cried Martin, shocked.

'Stop that madness!' I yelled.

Crunchie scowled at me. 'Don't listen to them, Padraic, you'll be the one laughing when you've got a belly full of chocolate cod.'

'Haha, I will indeed!' laughed Padraic.

'You will indeed what?' asked Martin, who couldn't see or hear Crunchie. (Martin was able to see other imaginaries like Bruce or the Magpie, but never another person's IF presumably because they stay hidden inside other people's heads, like brain nits.)

'Are you sure Crunchie's thought this one through?' queried Martin. 'Cos it really looks like you're just throwing good sweets into the river.'

'Yeah, it does kinda feel like that,' conceded Padraic.

Martin put an arm around his friend's shoulder and led him away a few paces. 'Hey, listen, P-Bone, have you ever thought of trading in Crunchie for a new IF? Cos I happen to have a spare one at the moment and could do you a great deal.'

Padraic's eyes lit up. 'Yes, please! I've always wanted a lanky, beardy one!'

'Er, no. My other IF. Loopy Lou.'

Padraic's smile faded a bit. 'Loopy Lou, your really annoying IF who's been driving you demented?'

'That's the one!'

'Does he still come with a chocolate fish?' he asked hopefully.

'No, I think he only had one of those, and it escaped down the toilet.'

'Right.' Padraic nodded. 'Then I think I'm going to have to say no.'

'Aw, come on, P! Help me out here! If I don't get rid of Lou, then they're going to evict Sean! I don't know what I'm going to do – everything's going all wrong!'

'Really? Your bully plans too?' asked Padraic, concerned.

'Actually, no – those are going quite well now,' replied Martin, perking up. 'Declan's taking Trisha to the pictures tonight, and with a bit of luck, he'll feel her boobs and be my bully protector forever.'

'Wow!' said Padraic, amazed. 'That's really nice of Trisha to help you out like that.'

'Er. Yeah.' Martin nodded vaguely.

'Sometimes when you ask for someone's help, they can really surprise you,' marvelled Padraic. 'That's why I always say – honesty is the best policy.'

'It is. It really is.' Martin nodded again, and we shared a guilty look.

Padraic could see that he was lying. 'She has no clue, does she?'

'No.'

'That makes more sense,' said Padraic. 'Well, don't worry, pal – I'm sure this is all going to work out great.'

'Really? You think so?'

'Well, either that, or it's going to be a total disaster.'

'That's reassuring,' I murmured.

But Martin brightened. 'You know what, Padraic? You're right. This has a fifty-per-cent chance of working out great! And that's almost two-thirds of one hundred per cent! I don't know what I've been worrying about! Thanks, P-Bag, you wise old buzzard.'

'Oh, don't thank me, Martin,' replied Padraic bashfully. 'You're the traveller. I'm merely a signpost on your journey.'

Martin frowned, a bit unclear.

'I'm a Traveller now?'

'So what am I?' asked Crunchie, wandering over.

'You're another signpost,' Padraic told him. 'Or maybe a bin or something.'

'A bin!' beamed Crunchie excitedly. 'The Keeper of the Rubbish! The Garbage Guardian! Lord of the Litter!'

# CHAPTER TWENTY-EIGHT
## SCUPPERED

It turned out that Padraic's peculiar pep talk was exactly what Martin needed, because by the time we got home he was more determined than ever to see his plans through. He marched into Trisha's room and triumphantly informed her that the date was on. He then opened her wardrobe and started to select an appropriate outfit for her to wear. After this he cowered on the floor, clutching his head where she had whacked him, and then crawled, less triumphantly, out of the room.

However, a few hours later, Trisha was all dolled up and ready to go. By 'dolled up', of course I mean she looked like a scary voodoo doll, and Martin was a little disappointed to see her swabbing black varnish all over her fingernails. But he'd learned his lesson by now and kept his 'fashion suggestions' to himself.

'Well, you look simply ravishing!' he told her.

Trisha rolled her eyes and continued to ready herself for the big date.

Martin and I watched happily. Yes, things were really falling into place now. By the end of the evening she'd officially be Mannion's Lady Friend, and Mannion would be Martin's Bully Protector. No more wedgies, no more Chinese burns, no more dead legs – apart from the ones he got from Sinead obviously, but that was a battle for another day.

Yes, we'd really done it. Like the good ship *Titanic*, this plan was utterly unsinkable.

'I'm a flippin' genius!' the boy sang, as we skipped down the hallway together like giddy schoolgirls.

'What's that, Martin?' asked Mammy Moone,

who we'd not noticed was walking behind us. 'How are you a genius?'

Martin racked his genius brain to come up with a decent lie.

'I just invented . . . toilet . . . roll . . . holders.'

'What on earth are you talking about?' she quizzed. 'Ya know what, Martin? You've been acting very odd lately. Is there something going on with you? Did you fall into a tree again?'

'All right, buddy,' I chipped in. 'Your lies aren't working wonderfully. Maybe you should try out Padraic's honesty theory?'

'Hmm . . . seems risky at this late stage,' the mini-Moone whispered back.

'What's risky, Martin? Who are you talking to?' his mam nagged. 'Have you been eating out-of-date Monster Mulch again?'

Martin took a deep breath and decided to try this new tactic.

'Oh . . . it's nothing, Mam. It's just . . . remember I had that little problem with the bullies at school?'

'Of course I do . . . Wait, they're not still picking on you, are they? Ya poor unfortunate eejit—'

'No, Mam, that's the thing. I don't think they're ever gonna pick on me ever again. I sorted it out.'

'*You* sorted it out?'

'Like a baby's jigsaw. I just came up with a simple solution, and took care of my problems like a man.'

Debra took Martin's little face in her hands and squeezed his cheeks like a day-old balloon.

'I'm so proud of you, sweetheart! I knew you'd come good eventually.'

Martin frowned, unsure what that meant.

'You *are* a flippin' genius.' She laughed. 'I knew if you put your mind to it, you'd be well able to take care of those eejits.'

'Thanks, Mam, but I actually put two minds to it.'

'Oh, so your dad helped you?'

'Oh no – he said he would, but I think he

just went to the pub instead.'

Debra frowned at the thought of her well-oiled other half.

'Well, at least there's one clever chap in this house.' She smiled, heading into the kitchen. 'C'mon, I'm making you congratulatory pancakes!'

'Pancakes!' I chirped. 'On a Saturday night?! It's like Las Vegas* in here!'

'I know, Sean. This honesty thing is working like a dream. I should've tried it years ago.' Martin beamed as he entered the kitchen.

'A glass of chocolate milk for the clever clogs?' Debra asked as she prepared the pancake batter.

'Why not? I've earned it.' Martin nodded.

'So how'd ya do it, Martin? How'd you finally get those bully brothers off your back?' Mam marvelled, like a wide-eyed student.

*LAS VEGAS - a magical city of lights, found in the American desert. Like discovering a diamond in a sandpit. If the diamond was fake. And smelled of wee.

Martin looked at me, wondering whether to continue down the truth trail.

I shrugged confidently. 'So far so good.'

'Well, Mother dear,' Martin boasted, as he slurped his choccie milk, 'I just used Trisha's boobs as bait.'

Debra stopped battering and lowered her whisk.

'Excuse me?' she muttered, turning slowly to face her son.

'I JUST USED TRISHA'S BOOBS AS BAIT!' Martin shouted, trying to make up for his mother's old ears.

We quickly realized her hearing was fine and that perhaps our plan might not have gone over so well. When we heard the sound of footsteps thundering towards the kitchen from the four corners of the house, we knew it hadn't.

'Any chance we finished that time machine, buddy?' I asked hopefully.

Before Martin could answer, the faces of

Trisha, Sinead, Fidelma and Liam appeared in the kitchen doorway like livid llamas*.

'You what!?' Martin's father demanded.

'Well . . .' the boy started, 'tonight I'm bribing a bully with a squeeze of my middle sister's chest sacks. Like . . . a genius?'

'Like flip you are,' Trisha snorted. 'My boobs get felt on my own terms.' Liam and Debra shared a look of concern as they watched Trisha high-five Fidelma before returning to her room for the night.

'Trisha, wait!' Martin blurted out in hope. 'He'll bring soup!'

'Martin, do you have any idea how much trouble you're in?' Liam boomed.

'Little to none?' the boy replied.

'Well, it's hard to blame him . . .' Debra argued. 'Apparently his dad was going to help him, but he went to the pub instead.'

Liam stared daggers at his tale-telling son.

*LIVID LLAMAS – terribly dangerous creatures with buck teeth and crooked feet. Also a chirpy pop duo from Peru.

'That's not . . . Well . . . It's complicated,' he sputtered.

As Martin's parents went off quarrelling, it was left to me to make some sense of our truth test.

'Well, I think it's safe to say that honesty is the *worst* policy, yeah?' I reasoned.

'You are *sooo* grounded!' Sinead shrilled, as she bounced away happily to the sitting room.

Martin suddenly imagined Declan and the Bonners on their way to the cinema, and how angry they'd be to find nothing but overpriced popcorn and a pretty man with hairdressing limbs.

'Worth one last go?' I queried, nodding towards the only sister left in the kitchen.

Martin took a deep breath, like the final passenger of the *Titanic*.

'Fidelma, . . . ya know the way you have boobs . . . ?'

A little later, Martin sat on his bed, nursing a black eye, filled with despair. After all

312

our careful planning, everything had been scuppered. On his copybook he'd written a simple, sad formula:

No date =no boob Feeling —bully proTecTor + seah getting eviCTed FRom my imaginATion = back To wheRe I FlippiN' STARTed

'Well, at least you're getting better at maths,' I noted.

He sighed glumly and closed his copybook.

'Aw, don't worry, buddy. We'll think of a new plan – a new and better plan!'

'Agreed.' Martin nodded. 'Cos we really can't go to school on Monday without a new plan.'

'No way. We absolutely need a new plan, and we've got all day Sunday to come up with it. That's oodles of plan-making time! We'll spend the first third of the day solving the bully problem and the second third of the day solving the eviction crisis.'

'Sounds perfect, Sean! That leaves us more than half a day to finalize the blueprints for my space-monkey factory!'

## Things we did on Sunday:

- played draughts
- Ate some Readybix
- Braided each other's hair
- Played Hide-and-Seek Ultra
- Found a Ladybird
- Built her a house
- Had a cup of tea
- Came back to find Ladybird's house collapsed
- Gave Ladybird a funeral
- Ate more Readybix
- Watched MacGyver
- Had a long lecture from mam and dad about boob respect and privacy

## Things we didn't do on Sunday:

- Come up with a new plan.

# CHAPTER TWENTY-NINE
# THE BALE-IFS

'Martin!' screeched his mam from the kitchen. 'Get up, ya lazy lump! You'll be late for school!'

Martin gave a sudden snort and sat upright in bed with his copybook stuck to his face. I was curled up on the floor, sleeping soundly, when he yanked the copybook off his forehead and flung it at me. 'Sean, wake up, ya lazy lump!'

I leaped to my feet, ready for anything (but hoping for breakfast).

'It's Monday, Sean! It's flippin' Monday!'

'Monday!' I cried with joy. 'I love Mondays!'

'No, Sean! It's Eviction Day! Plus I still don't have my Bully Protector – so we're both done for!'

'Well, that's a bit of a downer.' I frowned. 'Particularly after all that happy Monday talk.'

'What are we going to do?' he asked in a panic.

'Wait – didn't we stay up all night and come up with a new plan?'

'Did we?'

'Didn't we . . . ?'

'I don't remember. I hope we didn't come up with a load of great ideas and forget to write them down again,' said a panicking Martin.

'You mean like that time we came up with a way to send mail around the world through computers? By stuffing a letter inside a computer and then posting it?'

'Yes! Or that handy device we invented that mixes telephones with super-computers to create massive coin-operated super-phones?'

I snapped my fingers with frustration. 'Argh, if only we could remember the details! We'd be thousandaires* by now!'

*THOUSANDAIRES – like millionaires, but a little poorer and a lot flashier.

'Let's make a note to make notes from now on,' noted Martin.

'Noted. But I'm pretty sure we wrote it down this time.' I grabbed the copybook from the floor and whipped it open. 'See? We totally wrote it down! We're saved!'

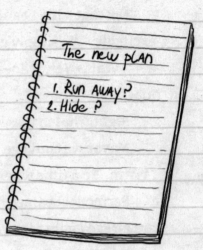

The new plan

1. Run Away?
2. Hide?

Martin looked at his scrawls on the copybook and then sighed sadly. 'Oh balls.'

A little later, we were on the road and getting closer to school by the minute, but were no closer to a solution.

'What if we fake our own deaths?' I suggested.

'Brilliant!' said Martin enthusiastically. 'How will we do that?'

'No idea,' I told him honestly.

He nodded glumly. 'What if we go

back in time?' he asked.

'Genius!' I cried. 'So long as it doesn't require a time machine.'

'No, that's the beauty of it!' he exclaimed excitedly. 'We simply go back in time using a . . . Wait – Yes, it does. It requires a time machine.'

'Right. That makes it trickier.'

'Maybe we could go *forward* in time,' mused Martin. 'To a time when we're safe!'

'Perfect!' I beamed. 'The thing is though, we are already going forward in time.'

'Even better!'

'Yeah. It's just . . . I don't think we can go any faster than this though.'

'Right,' nodded Martin, seeing the problem. 'Well, that's not very helpful then, is it?'

We both sighed and continued to trudge down the road, stumped, when suddenly the stumpy figure of Loopy Lou rolled out of a bush beside us.

'Loopy Lou in da house!' he yelled, and

tumbled into a damp pothole. 'Aw, nuts!' he cried, then clambered to his feet, wiping the muck from his coat.

'Hi, Lou,' said Martin.

Lou stopped wiping and beamed at him. 'Peekaboo, Marty Moo! Where you two sneaky-sneaks been hiding?'

Martin shrugged. 'Just at my house.'

'Your house!' shouted Lou, annoyed with himself. 'Knew I should've checked there.'

'So do you fancy another game of hide-and-seek, Lou?' I asked.

'Ha!' scoffed Lou. 'I'm not gonna fall for that one again! No more games, beardo! Time's up! It's Eviction Day!'

'Not even a quick game of charades?' I suggested.

'Oh, I love charades!' Martin smiled eagerly.

'I've got a charade for you!' Lou snapped at me. 'Two words. Five syllables. "Get him, boys!"'

'Is it a film?' Martin frowned, confused.

Just then I noticed two well-built, menacing-looking figures advancing down the road towards us. They were moving quickly, cracking their knuckles, and were clearly ready for a fight.

'Oh balls,' I whimpered, getting a sinking feeling in my stomach. 'They've sent the Bale-IFs.'

'The bailiffs*?' asked Martin.

'The Hay Brothers,' I cried. 'The toughest IFs in the whole imaginary kingdom.'

'Righty-roo, Seanie-poo!' Lou giggled maniacally.

Martin turned to see the tough-looking thugs storming towards us. Ronnie Hay and Reggie Hay were large, hulking, identical twins. They wore black bomber jackets and had cold expressions, like a couple of hardened hit men.

*BAILIFFS – big burly men who throw people out of their homes for not paying their bills. History's most famous bailiff is of course the Big Bad Wolf from the Battle of the Three Little Piggies.

The gruesome two-some were basically the Bonner Brothers of the imaginary world. Apart from all the hay. Oh yes, at this point I should probably also mention that they were bales of hay. Which might not sound very scary. But if you've ever been beaten up by a pair of bomber-jacket-wearing hay thugs, then you'll know differently. The folks from C.L.I.F.F. sometimes hired the pair to take care of their dirty business for them. So I guess I was now that dirty business. A skid mark on the road that the Hays were about to wipe out.

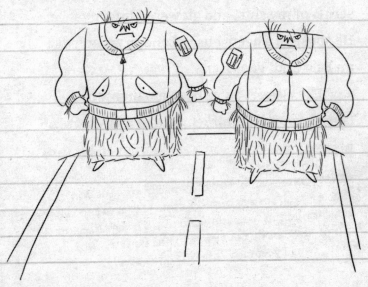

'They don't look pleasant,' observed Martin. 'What do they want?'

'What do you think? They want to evict me! We gotta get out of here!'

'So they're bailiffs?'

'Yes, that's what I said! Bale-IFs!'

I was eager to escape, but Martin was still jabbering. 'Wait, are you saying "bailiffs" or "Bale-IFs"?'

'What does it matter? Run, ya idiot!'

But it was too late – the Hay Brothers were already upon us. Ronnie Hay grabbed me by the scruff of my shirt and glowered into my face. He spoke in a deep, husky London accent, like an East End* gangster.

''Ello, Sean. You've been a naugh'y boy, 'aven't you?' He smirked, with a crazy look in his eye.

*EAST END – the gritty part of London, where gangsters come from. It's also where art students parade around in home-made clogs and controversial haircuts, which must really annoy the gangsters.

'Have I?' I squeaked.

'Yes, you 'ave, Sean.'

'Yes, he flippin' has!' Reggie Hay grinned.

'You been very naugh'y indeed, Sean,' continued Ronnie. 'You been illegally occupyin' this boy's imagination. 'Aven't you?'

'Have I?' I whimpered.

'Yes, you 'ave, Sean,' he growled.

'He flippin' has!' chirped Reggie. He sounded delighted.

'You've become quite the problem,' continued Ronnie. 'And you know what we do with problems?'

'Treat them gently?' I asked hopefully.

Ronnie leaned closer. 'We make 'em go away,' he said ominously.

Just then I realized that Martin wasn't beside me any more. During this chilling chat, he'd managed to sneak around behind the Hays and was now on his hands and knees right behind their feet.

'Whatcha doin', Marty?' asked Lou curiously. 'Pretending to be a moo-moo?'

But Martin ignored the moron. 'Shove them, Sean!' he yelled.

And I didn't hesitate for a single moment! OK, I may have hesitated for several moments because I was quite terrified. But eventually I swallowed my fears and gave the Hays an almighty shove, sending them toppling back over Martin.

'Haha!' I cried triumphantly. But we didn't have much time to enjoy our victory, as they were already clambering to their feet and now looked angrier than ever.

'You're gonna regret that, Seanie-boy,' growled Ronnie Hay.

Martin and I scrambled over a hedge into a grassy field. We bolted across it, but the brothers were racing after us, hot on our heels, shedding hay as they ran.

Just then I spotted a flock of sheep huddled in the middle of the field and got an idea. 'Martin! Lead them into the sheep! It's our only hope!'

We swerved towards the sheep, and as soon as the furry beasts saw the hay bales approaching they got very excited, bleating hungrily. 'Hey, look, it's hay! Aw, I'm dyin' for a nice bit of hay.'

Martin and I sprinted through the flock, but when the Bale-IFs tried to follow, the sheep blocked their path, surrounding them, nibbling at the hay.

'C'mere!' they bleated. 'Ya smell lovely. Do you taste lovely?'

'Out of the way, stupid sheep!' yelled Ronnie Hay.

'Stop nibblin' me!' snapped Reggie Hay, and whacked a sheep on the nose.

It took the brothers a while to wade through the hungry flock, and by then we were out of sight.

Loopy Lou was not impressed. 'You goofy goons! They gots away!'

In the distance, Martin and I watched them from behind a bush.

'You know, you really are superb at running away, Martin,' I told him.

'You're not too shabby yourself, Sean!'

We high-fived each other happily and then did what we did best – continued to run away.

# CHAPTER THIRTY
## THE FINAL WRECKONING!

Martin and I were still running when we reached his school. We bolted through the front gates and hid behind a wall. As well as being great running-awayers, we were excellent hiders.

The Hay brothers were nowhere to be seen. But we knew we weren't out of the woods yet.

'Well, Martin, we've managed to escape our imaginary foes, but we still have our real enemies to contend with,' I whispered.

'The flippin' Bonner brothers!' he remembered gravely.

'Yeah, and I'm sure Declan Mannion isn't going to be too pleased that Trisha never showed up last night either.'

'He's probably going to beat me up himself, isn't he?'

'Probably.' I nodded. 'Hey, I've got an idea!'

'About flippin' time. Is it any good?'

'Yeah, I mean . . . it's pretty complicated, but if we get it right, it just might work!'

'Spill the beans, beard-face!'

'Let's just keep running away.'

Martin considered my complex plan for three full seconds.

'That's brilliant, Sean! Let's just run away from our problems forever,' he exclaimed, retying his shoelaces in readiness.

'But where shall we go?' I wondered.

'Let's head west, Sean. We'll hit China in no time!'

'You're the geography nut,' I agreed, and we high-fived and jumped to our feet, excited for our Far Western adventure.

We turned in unison and ran straight into Declan Mannion.

*Gulp.*

'Steady your pace, Moone-face,' Declan grunted, after Martin had rebounded off his chest.

'Heeeey, Declan . . . you . . . look extra strong today . . .' Martin started, unsure what to say.

'Think quick, buddy, and remember – honesty is the *worst* policy,' I reminded him.

'So . . . about last night . . . I don't suppose you saw that tornado that hit a very small area of Boyle . . .'

'Wha—? Wait . . . Was I supposed to go to the cinema last night?'

'WE'RE FREE!' I whooped. 'He forgot!'

'Oh . . . no, Declan,' Martin lied. 'I was just

making small talk. People love talking about the weather, don't they?'

'No.' Declan shrugged as he started to move away.

'Listen, Mr Mannion . . .' Martin called. 'I have a feeling I might need your help today. Any chance I could get an advance on my bully protection?'

Declan shook his head. 'Sorry, Moone, but I cannot aid, for the booby price has not yet been paid,' he said as he sauntered off towards the bike sheds for a smoke.

'All right, buddy. Let's get this show on the road,' I suggested.

'Moone!' We turned to find Jonner and Conor Bonner stomping towards us like a pair of T. rex shadows.

His brother grinned. 'The very man.'

'Hi, lads.' Martin smiled nervously.

'We owe you a Bonner beatin'*,'

*A BONNER BEATIN' – a rural type of sibling assault. It's a bit muckier than a standard beating, with more cursing, and usually ends with a double-dunk into a cowpat.

Jonner Bonner informed him.

'A Bonner beatin'. . .?'

Conor nodded. 'We waited outside the cinema for three hours last night. We got chilly.'

'*Real* chilly,' Jonner added.

'Right. Well, er . . . I'm not sure I can fit you in right now, lads. Let me check my schedule—'

'Here's the schedule, Moone,' interrupted Jonner Bonner, raising his fists.

Martin winced, thinking he was about to get thumped, but then saw that there was something written across Jonner's knuckles.

'Wow, that's very organized of you,' said Martin, genuinely impressed. 'It's like a fist-list.'

'Fists aren't just for fightin',' Jonner explained.

'They're for knocking too!' said Conor, and rapped on Martin's head with his knuckles.

'Ow!'

'Right, let's start fightin',' said Jonner Bonner, as he and his brother grabbed Martin and put him into a double headlock.

'Argh!' he struggled helplessly.

'OK, don't panic,' I reassured him. 'I've got another idea! An idea that might just kill two birds with one stone. Which is kind of ironic, since this all started when we were trying to *save* a bird—'

'Spit it out, Sean!' yelled Martin frantically.

'Give Loopy Lou to the Bonners!' I cried.

'Who ya talkin to?' snapped Conor Bonner. 'We told ya before! No talkin' when we're fightin' ya! It totally puts us off!'

'Sorry, lads,' apologized Martin, thinking fast. 'I was just, er . . . talking to, er . . . my imaginary friend, Loopy Lou!'

'Your what?'

The Bonners paused and peered at him.

'Do ye not have imaginary friends?' scoffed Martin, as if they were far behind the trend. 'Ah, lads, you're missing out.'

'Where is he?' demanded Conor Bonner, glancing around uneasily.

'Over there.' Martin gestured with a nod of his head.

Conor Bonner swung a wild punch. 'Did I hit him?'

'No, he's over here now.'

Conor Bonner reeled around and threw another jab into thin air. 'Am I getting closer?'

'No, he's like a ninja,' bragged Martin, clearly still focused on getting to Asia. 'You'd never beat him at fighting.'

Their eyes lit up. 'A ninja? We flippin' love ninjas*!'

Martin pounced on the opportunity. 'Well, how about we make a trade then? You never beat me up again, and I'll give him to you!'

The Bonners looked at each other, considering it.

'What kind of ninja is he?' asked Jonner Bonner. 'A jumpy one? Or a stabby one?'

'He's, er . . .'

'Careful, Martin,' I said, remembering what Bruce had told us in the woods. 'They have to imagine Lou like he is. That's the only way he can make the leap from *your* imagination to *their* imaginations.'

'He's, er . . .' continued Martin, less confidently, 'er . . . kind of . . . an overweight ninja. And, er . . . he doesn't really wear ninja

*NINJAS - very quiet people who sneak around in black dressing gowns - they're basically like monks, but more murderous.

334

clothes. His outfit is more a medley of polka dots and clown shoes. But he's great fun,' Martin insisted. 'Great gas altogether. Goes by the name of Loopy Lou.'

The Bonners seemed confused. 'So he's not a ninja?'

'Er, no. Not in the traditional sense. He's closer to being a sort of clown really. Like a sort of . . . annoying, really needy clown,' he explained honestly. 'So you want him?' he asked eagerly.

The Bonners did not look impressed. 'Let's get back to fightin',' said Jonner.

The brothers were just about to put Martin back into the double headlock when suddenly he spotted the new boy, Trevor, sitting nearby. Since the Bonners spent most days fast asleep at the back of the class, they hadn't yet noticed this new kid, and Martin couldn't think of a better time to introduce them.

'Hey look, lads. A new fella!' he cried, pointing at Trevor.

'A new fella?' they frowned, their eyes darting around for him. They zipped up their jackets menacingly, ready for action. Martin knew that there was nothing bullies liked more than fresh meat, and Trevor was just sitting there like a freshly baked steak sarnie*.

*SARNIE – another word for sandwich. Sandwiches were famously invented by the Earl of Sandwich, who was a distant cousin of the Duchess of Poptarts.

## CHAPTER THIRTY-ONE
## THE IMAGINARY TRANSPLANT

Martin waved to Trevor to come and join them.
He hurried over happily in his clean jumper
with his combed hair and his snotless face. He
gave a warm, friendly smile and stuck out his
hand for them to shake.

'Hi, I'm Trevor.' He beamed at the Bonners.
'I don't believe we've met. What're your names,
new pals?'

The boys looked at him blankly for a
moment. Then Jonner Bonner grabbed his
hand and pulled him into a tight grip,
pinning him rigid. Conor Bonner began to
pummel the newbie as Martin scurried away,
like a coward.

At the doors of the school, Martin paused
and looked back. He couldn't help but feel partly

responsible for Trevor's misfortune. 'I feel bad,' he told me glumly.

'Aw, don't beat yourself up about it, Marty,' I said, trying to lift his spirits. 'It's really Trevor's fault – for being new.'

Martin considered this theory as we looked back at Trevor, who was trying to smile his way through the beatin'. But his eyes weren't smiling. They were blinking. And frowning. And starting to leak a little.

'I don't know, Sean, it's making me feel funny. Funny in the ol' blood pumper.' Martin pressed his heart.

'That's guilt, my friend. And there's only one way to stop it, I'm afraid.'

We looked at each other and nodded knowingly. In that moment Martin Moone decided to be heroic for the first time in his idiotic little life.

He pushed his chest out, stood tall and marched towards the Bonner brothers purposefully.

'Stop!!!'

*BRRRRRriiiiiiiiiiiinnnnnnngggggggg.*

Just then the school bell went.

The Bonners looked at Martin, confused.

'Er . . . ye'll be late for class, lads,' Martin
suggested.

The brothers looked at each other.

'Well, we wouldn't want that,' Jonner said, to
our surprise.

'Nope, lateness is not on the schedule today,'
added Conor as he dropped Trevor to the ground
and held up his fists.

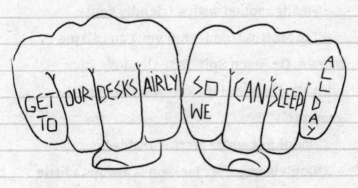

'Don't worry new fella, we'll pick up this
beatin' later,' Conor assured Trevor as he
headed inside to fall asleep at his desk.

'And every morning for the rest of your life,' added Jonner happily, pulling a pillow from his schoolbag.

As kids flooded through the school doors like weary waves, Martin and I sighed with relief. We looked to the newbie, still dusting himself off on the tarmac*.

'Hey, Trevor,' said Martin brightly.

Trevor looked up in surprise. He glanced behind him to see if there was another Trevor sitting there, but he was alone. Someone was actually talking to him.

'Hi,' he replied with a friendly smile.

'I'm Martin Moone. But you can call me Martin. Or Peach Spit. Actually, let's stick with Martin. Mind if I join you there on the ground?'

'Shouldn't we be getting inside?'

'Don't worry – Mr Jackson is always a little

*TARMAC – like cement. A type of tar laid by Irish fellas. They're usually called MacCarthy or MacDonell, hence the Mac bit.

late on Mondays. And very late the rest of the week,' Martin said as he sat down beside him. 'Sorry about the Bonners. Are ya OK?'

Trevor nodded sadly. 'Yeah. So I guess there's bullies in Roscommon too.'

'Ah, they're everywhere. Like flippin' werewolves.'

'Haven't noticed any werewolves around . . .'

'Aw, that's just it. You never notice them until it's too late. And then . . . boom! You've been wedgied.'

Trevor gave an uncertain nod.

'How ya settling in apart from that?' asked Martin.

Trevor shrugged. 'OK, I suppose.'

Declan Mannion passed by on his way from the bike sheds and shouted at Trevor. 'Stupid flippin' newbie!'

Trevor half waved back, as Declan sauntered off.

'It's not exactly the *friendliest* school though.'

Martin looked down, a little ashamed. 'No, I suppose not.'

'To be honest, I could really do with a good friend, Martin. Ya know?'

When Trevor said this, Martin started feeling a motion in his thinking jelly. He turned to me.

'A wingman,' continued Trevor. 'A best bud. You know what I mean?'

'Yes, I do know!' Martin blurted in reply, sharing an excited look with me. 'You need a male companion!'

'Exactly! Or any kind of companion really.' He shrugged again. 'I'm not picky.'

'He's perfect!' I beamed, delighted. 'We've finally found our guy!'

'Maybe *you* could be my friend, Martin,' suggested Trevor earnestly.

Martin put a hand on his shoulder and said honestly, 'I would love that, Trevor.'

Trevor's face lit up. 'You would?'

'But I've got an even better idea!' continued Martin. 'How about an *imaginary* friend?'

Trevor's smile faltered slightly. 'But . . . wouldn't a real friend be better?'

'Pfff,' I snorted, shaking my head. 'Idiot.'

'Real friends are OK,' Martin explained, 'but imaginary friends are way better! I mean, can a real friend do this?'

He pointed at me and I pulled a crazy-looking face that was simply hilarious. Martin roared with laughter, but since Trevor couldn't actually see me, he just seemed slightly confused. 'Er . . . no?'

'No, they can't!' agreed Martin emphatically. 'Imaginary friends are the best! And today's your lucky day, Trevor! Because I've got just the one for you!'

He hopped to his feet, barely able to contain his excitement. This was our best chance yet of getting rid of Loopy Lou, and Martin was determined to nail it. But unfortunately he didn't have much experience as a salesman. So, not knowing what else to do, he suddenly launched into a song.

*Picture a man, a magical man.*
*A magical imaginary man!*
*He's jolly and gentle and a little bit mental,*
*He's a flabby, fantastical man!*

*He's happy-go-lucky, he plays the kazoo!*
*He's dumb like a puppy,*
*     but knows where to poo.*
*He's bouncy and bald,*
*     he's loyal and he's true,*
*And his name is Loopy Loopington Lou!*

With those final words, Martin thrust out his arms theatrically, and froze in a final dramatic pose.

'Wow,' I murmured, a little taken aback. 'That was unexpected.'

But then suddenly Trevor burst into applause, clearly won over by Martin's silly song. And applause came from behind us too.

'Oh, Marty!' cried Loopy Lou, wiping away a tear. 'That's the sweetest thing anyone's ever sung about me! I'm blubbering like a blubber-donkey*!'

'Wait! What the flip is Lou doing here?!' I shrieked. I sprang to my feet and tried to flee, but the Bale-IFs were already upon me.

'Oh no, you don't,' whispered Ronnie Hay into my ear.

'You're nicked!' announced his brother with a grin.

'Lemme go!' I yelled, struggling to get free, but the Bale-IFs hauled me away.

'Hey, go easy there, Hay-hoos!,' said Lou, feeling a little bad for me.

But the Hays paid no attention and dragged me away as Martin looked on in horror.

'NOOOOO!' he cried.

'You all right there, Moone?' called Mr Jackson, who was slowly and tardily sauntering

*BLUBBER-DONKEY – a rare beast that is the offspring of a whale and a donkey. Spends a lot of time crying. Because it can never find clothes that fit.

towards the school. He could see neither me, Lou nor the Bale-IFs, so was a little confused by Martin's outburst.

'Yep. Grand.' Martin waved stupidly. 'Just . . . shouting "No".'

'Do it, Martin!' I called as they hauled me off. 'Do it now! It's our only hope!'

Martin nodded and turned back to Trevor. 'So you want an imaginary friend?' he asked, with some urgency.

'Yeah, he sounds fun all right.' Trevor nodded. 'But maybe he should have big angel wings too!' he added excitedly. 'So he can fly around and shoot lightning—'

'What? No, he doesn't have wings!'

'Quickly, Martin!' I yelped.

'Or how about spider legs!' suggested Trevor eagerly. 'Or maybe a weird humped back!' He grinned.

'What?!' asked Martin in a panic. 'No, stop making stuff up! He looks normal! Kinda!'

'But if he's imaginary, why can't I make him

more special?' asked Trevor reasonably.

'Cos that's not who he is!' snapped Martin.

He glanced over at Lou, who was watching me getting dragged roughly out of the playground. Even Lou looked quite concerned, biting his fingertips, which made the boy even more nervous.

'He's basically just a big balding overweight oaf,' said Martin honestly. 'And he can be pretty annoying sometimes. But all he wants is to be the best imaginary friend ever. And he needs a realsie who'll look after him, and appreciate him, and not fire him or send him to the sea or abandon him in the woods. He needs a better realsie than me,' Martin admitted. 'He needs a realsie who really wants him.'

Trevor's eyes glazed over as he imagined Loopy Lou. And nearby, Loopy Lou suddenly began to glow. He turned around, frowning, looking at his body that was now shimmering magically.

He looked to Martin, concerned. 'Marty Moo . . . ? What you do?'

347

Martin looked to Trevor. 'So . . . do ya want him?'

All eyes turned to the newbie.

'You bet I flippin' do!' cried Trevor.

And with that, Lou vanished from Martin's imagination with a POP!

In that same moment, Trevor's face lit up as he welcomed his new friend into his head. Martin couldn't see Lou any more, but Trevor was soon chatting away to him.

'Loopy like a fruity loop! Haha! What a brilliant rap song. Do it again! I could never hear that song enough!'

Martin Moone had successfully performed an imaginary transplant. And now there was no need for me to be evicted – he'd saved me!

He turned around to tell me the good news, but I was nowhere to be seen. He sprinted over to where he'd last seen me, but the Bale-IFs and I had disappeared. There was nothing left but an empty red hat.

'Sean!' he cried. 'Where are you?'

But there was no reply.

As Trevor headed inside, whistling a happy song, Martin was left behind with tears in his eyes, crushed.

He'd taken too long to do the transplant. He was too late, and I was gone. Just like Loopy Lou and the Bale-IFs.

For the first time since this whole adventure began, Martin's imagination was completely empty. In the course of a single morning he'd gone from having two imaginary friends to having none, and he'd never felt more alone.

## CHAPTER THIRTY-TWO
## READYBIX-TO-GO

Several days passed. Several lonely, imaginary-friend-less days. Every morning, Martin would wake up and expect to find me there, curled up on the floor like his faithful badger. But every morning, all that lay on the floor were Readybix crumbs, saggy scrunchies and bits of Sinead's flaky skin.

Each day at school, Martin would ask Padraic if Crunchie Haystacks had heard anything about me. But the answer was always the same.

'Sorry, pal. Still nothing.'

Then one day Padraic told him that I'd escaped! Crunchie had heard that I'd overpowered the Bale-IFs and gone on the run. He said that I was a stowaway on a steamship bound for the Himalayas* and was going to start a new life as a sherpa*. But when pressed for more details, Crunchie confessed that he'd simply made this all up.

'Sorry, pal,' Padraic apologized to Martin. 'Crunchie just got bored of telling me the same thing every day.'

Martin nodded sadly.

It was like I'd simply vanished without a trace. And all Martin had to remember me by was his red woolly hat. And *my* red woolly hat. He'd mixed them up and couldn't remember which one was which. So he treasured them both and wore them day and night.

*HIMALAYAS – home to the Abominable Snowman. It's also home to the Abominable Scarecrow, who is actually way more abominable, but is less well-known as he's always covered in snow and doesn't move so no one ever sees him.

*SHERPA – an expert at mountaineering, who guides explorers through mountains. The Irish equivalent is the Designated Donkey, who guides drunken farmers home from the pub through the hills.

But Martin couldn't just sit around wearing hats. He was now a man of action and needed to do something. So he decided to make a bunch of 'Missing' posters and stick them up around town. He carefully drew a picture of me, but then remembered that to everyone else I was invisible. So he wisely changed it to an invisible drawing of me.

But all his hard work on the posters led to nothing, and life soon returned to its boring ways for Martin Moone. His sisters continued to torment him, as did the Bonners – but he avoided them all as best he could. He did all the usual stuff – he went to school and did his homework and watched TV and did his drawings and rode around town on his clunky rust-mobile.

But he couldn't shake the feeling that

something was missing. Something tall. And imaginary. And beardy.

A couple of weeks passed without any news, until one morning Martin opened his wardrobe and saw something lying at the bottom of it. It was an envelope! Envelopes are so exciting! It lay atop a pile of old shoes and Martin snatched it up. His name was scrawled on the front in my familiar handwriting, and he ripped it open eagerly.

Inside, he found a note.

MARTIN.
THE WOODS TOMORROW.
CAUTION!

The next morning, Martin hurried into the kitchen to find the rest of the Moones tucking into breakfast.

His mother looked up at him. 'Readybix?' she asked brightly.

'You say that as if there are other options, Mam,' grumbled Fidelma.

'Well, you could always have . . . no Readybix,' said Debra.

They all paused eating.

'That's an option?' asked Liam, who was forcing down his fourth bowl of the stuff.

'No,' admitted Debra. 'Eat up, gang.' She then picked up a clean bowl. 'Now, Martin. Nice and dusty?'

'Sure, Mam. But make it snappy, I've got to head off.'

'Head off where?' she asked.

Martin paused and remembered my wise words. 'Honesty is the worst policy,' I echoed from the past.

'Er. Nowhere . . . ?'

This seemed like a rock-solid answer, but for some reason they all looked at him suspiciously. But before they could interrogate him further, Martin was saved by a knock on the back door, and Padraic entered.

'Morning, Moones!' he waved.

The girls grunted at him with disdain.

'We should get going, M-Meister. You all set?'

'I am indeed, P-nut,' said Martin. 'Maybe I'll take that Readybix to-go, Mam.'

Debra turned to Padraic. 'Where are you off to?'

Padraic paused nervously. 'Er. Nowhere . . . ?' he replied.

Martin desperately tried to come up with a good lie. 'We're going to . . . a funeral!' he announced suddenly.

'A funeral?' asked his dad. 'For who?'

'No one you'd know,' Martin assured him.

'Yeah, just one of our friends.' Padraic nodded.

Debra looked alarmed. 'One of your friends died?'

'Ah no,' said Padraic. 'Just . . . part of him died. He lost a leg.'

'You're going to a funeral for your friend's leg?' asked Debra.

Martin chuckled nervously, sensing that this wasn't believable enough. 'Haha. No, no, I don't know why we said that. We're going to somewhere . . . totally normal.'

'His left leg I think he said it was!' cried Padraic.

'Haha, big stupid Padraic,' Martin laughed as he dragged his pal out the door with one arm and grabbed a couple of dry Readybix with the other. 'Right, well, we'd better hit the road. Loads of normal stuff to do before lunch. See ya!'

'Happy Saturday, Moones!' Padraic waved as they made their hasty escape.

Outside, Martin took his rusty old girls' bike and started to wheel the creaking crock towards the driveway. But then Liam came out after him.

'Hang on a sec, Martin!' he called. 'Almost forgot.'

He disappeared into his workshop for a moment and then re-emerged holding the Readybix bike. He carried it over to Martin.

'I managed to bash your new bike back into some kind of shape,' he said. 'Do you still want it?'

Martin looked at his bike and saw that Liam had done a lot of work on it. There were two new wheels and a patch on the saddle. And even though the frame was covered in countless little dings where Liam had banged the dents out of it, it looked fantastic.

'Look . . . I know it's not perfect, but, well . . . none of us is perfect. And I can't have my little man on a girl's bike. So I figured . . . if you're going to be running away from bullies, you might as well cycle away from them. And—'

He was about ramble on but Martin hugged him so tightly he had to shut up. Liam was a little taken aback by this, unsure what to do.

Then Padraic came up and wrapped his arms around both of them.

'Ahh. Nothing like a big, lovely man-hug in the morning,' sighed Padraic contentedly.

They held this awkward embrace for a few moments. 'Right,' said Liam finally. 'Well, you better head on, lads. I imagine it takes ages to get to somewhere totally normal.'

He winked at Martin, who smiled. Then the two boys hopped on their bikes and pedalled away, speeding down the driveway together with hope in their hearts and Readybix-to-go in their pockets.

# CHAPTER THIRTY-THREE
## A WHOLE LOAD OF SWEARING

> **Boyle, 4th November.**
> **Forecast: Chance of rain. Look – it's winter.**
>  **It's Ireland. If it doesn't rain,**
> **I'd blame global warming.**

'Thanks for coming with me, P-Bug,' said Martin,
as they strolled through the woods together.
'Just thought I could do with a wingman on
this one.'

'No problemo,' replied Padraic. 'I love
coming to the woods when primroses are out
of season. Hey, I was wondering – when Sean
signed that note "Caution", do you think he was
just writing his middle name, or was he actually
saying . . . BEWARE?'

'No idea.' Martin shrugged. 'But I'd say it

was definitely one of the two.'

Padraic nodded, looking a little worried.

They ventured into the dark depths of the woods until they eventually reached the clearing. Bruce the Spruce and Laurel the Laurel were blocking their path.

'Hi, lads,' waved Martin. 'I don't suppose you guys have seen Sean Murphy anywhere, have you? He's the one who used to be known as CustServRep263. Tall, probably looks lonely.'

The two trees turned to him and Bruce held up a clipboard. 'And your name ish?'

Martin looked a little taken aback, but then Bruce laughed. 'Haha! Jus' kidding. I no stoopid, I remember you! Trees no forget nothing! We're the elephants of the woods!'

'Ha! Because you both have trunks?' chuckled Padraic, eager to be part of the conversation.

Bruce stopped laughing and frowned. 'What? No, cos we both remember stuff. Trunks got nothing to do with it. Dis totally different kind of trunk.'

'Oh, right,' murmured Padraic apologetically.

'You tink dis look like elephant's trunk?' asked Bruce, slapping his chest with his twiggy hands.

'No, sir,' said Padraic, regretfully.

'Who's this langer, Martin?' asked Laurel, gesturing at Padraic. 'He another tree racist, is he?'

'This langer is Padraic,' Martin explained kindly.

Bruce ran a wooden finger down the list on his clipboard. 'Ah, here we go: "Martin's stoopid friend Padraic".'

'That's me!' chirped Padraic.

'OK, in you go, guys. Enjoy de show!'

'The show?' asked Martin. 'I'm just here to meet Sean.'

'Yesh, yesh, in you go, it's about to start. Wait a shec – are you boys OK with blood?'

The boys looked at him, concerned.

'Depends. Seeing it or drinking it?' asked Padraic.

'Whose blood?' asked Martin, uneasily.

'Well, Sean Murphy's, of course!' replied Bruce.

'Oh balls,' whispered Martin, looking quite alarmed.

But before Bruce could explain, there was a loud BONG!

'Quick, Brucey, it's about to start!' cried Laurel. 'Places, places, c'mon, ya langers!'

The two trees cantered away, leaving Martin looking very worried. He hurried into the clearing, followed by Padraic.

When they pushed through the branches into the wide open space, they paused to take in the scene before them.

It was November now, and everywhere else in the woods was bare and leafless – but here it was like the height of spring.

Wildflowers had sprouted everywhere, and the boys found themselves standing among a flood of bluebells and snowdrops and daffodils. And around the clearing, all the trees were in leaf, showing off their handsome colours of red and gold and blue. Yeah, that's right – blue! Mother Nature had pulled out all the stops.

The clearing was thronged with about a hundred imaginary friends – but of course Martin and Padraic couldn't actually see any of them. They could only see Bruce and Laurel, and a dopey-looking unicorn who stood beside the buffet, providing fresh juice for the punch bowl. The table was filled with canapés* and strange delicacies**.

*CANAPÉS – miniature food served at parties. The tiny portions are designed to make everyone feel like giants, and therefore more confident and chatty.

**DELICACIES – Disgusting things that rich people eat.

Just then, Laurel tapped a knife against his glass, making a tinkling noise.

'OK, quiet everybody, quiet!' yelled Bruce the Spruce. He and Laurel were standing by a little wooden gazebo* at one end of the clearing where a microphone stand was set up.

*WOODEN GAZEBO – basically a big wooden tent. Not ideal for hiking trips. Very tricky to fit into a backpack.

'Quiet, stoopids!' he yelled, and finally the clearing fell silent.

'Dis a great honour and everybody give a big whoopie whoopie to one of de most powerful creatures of the imaginary world. And I should know, because he poops me out every shingle day! Put your hands together for Ming the Magpie!'

The imaginary friends erupted into applause, which Martin and Padraic couldn't hear, but they could see Martin's old magpie friend, who fluttered down to the gazebo.

Ming landed on the microphone stand and tapped the mic with his beak. 'Hi, folks. This thing on?'

It made a piercing feedback noise and everyone cheered with amusement.

'Haha! OK, settle down,' said Ming, gesturing with his wings for quiet. 'Thanks a lot for coming, everybody. Great to see ya. Can't stay long, I'm afraid. Herself is not well. Upset tummy. Ate a dodgy maggot, I think.

Anyway, let's get on with it. Customer Service Representative 263749, where are ya?' he called, looking out at the crowd.

'Right here!' I replied, from behind Martin.

Martin turned, and his stupid little face lit up. 'Sean!'

'Hey, buddy. Miss me?'

'Come on up, big fella!' called Ming. 'And bring your realsie too.'

'What's happening, Sean?' Martin asked, worried.

'You'll see, buddy, you'll see.'

The crowd parted, and we made our way through all the other IFs – fairy godmothers, cowboys, robots, superheroes, overgrown rabbits, wrestlers, even some sort of giant blob. And among them all, I spotted Crunchie Haystacks and Loopy Lou.

'Lookin' spifferoo, Seanie-poo!' Lou gave me a thumbs up.

'Hi, Martin!' called Trevor beside him, who had just arrived too.

We waved back happily, and soon reached the gazebo.

Ming tapped the mic with his beak again. 'Right. Now, as many of ye know, Sean got evicted from this young lad's imagination because he wasn't a proper IF. But after our investigation, we've determined that Sean lived up to the ideals of imaginary friendship by helping Martin to deal with the Bonner brothers and also to perform an imaginary transplant, giving Loopy "Loopington" Lou to a kid who needed him more than anyone.'

I glanced back at Loopy Lou, who wiped away a tear and blew his nose loudly.

'And because of these noble deeds,' continued Ming, 'the C.L.I.F. has decided that Sean has proved himself as an IF. He may not be schooled in the arts, but he is as true and as loyal and as imaginary as anyone here. And so, I hereby declare that Customer Service Representative 263749, the imaginary clerk,

is today being upgraded, and will henceforth be known as Sean "Caution" Murphy, Imaginary Friend!'

The place erupted in applause, and Martin gave me a triumphant high five.

After the cheers died down, we got stuck into the formalities of the swearing-in ceremony. I bonged the Great Gong. I wore the Enchanted Duffle Coat, and Ming tapped me on the head seven times with the Sacred Spoon. I sipped some IFfy milk from the Ancient Goblet of IFfyness, puked a little and finally I was ready to take the Oath.

I faced the crowd and put my hand on my heart.

'I pledge allegiance to my realsie.

To be his friend and faithful figment.

To buck him up when he's down.

To help him down when he's up. (Stuck in a tree perhaps.)

To take part in all his schemes and adventures, even when they're doomed to failure and might actually land us in hospital or jail.

To never say, "No." Or, "Stop." Or, "I really wouldn't eat that if I were you."

To only say, "Yes." Or, "We should totally steal it!" Or, "Let's run, dumbo!"

But above all I pledge to be his faithful imaginary friend, from this day until the end of time.

Or at least until his teenage years, when he'll probably start kissing girls or get bored of me and stop imagining me or whatever.'

Ming gave a proud smile (at least I think he did – it's hard to tell with beaks) and then he led the crowd in the final ceremonial chant to seal the Oath.

'IFFY!' he shouted.

'I!' we all shouted back.

'IFFY!'

'I!'

'IFFY! IFFY! IFFY!'

'I! I! I!'

Once more the crowd erupted into whoops and cheers. And at last I was an official imaginary friend.

Well-wishers came forward, patting me on the back and congratulating me.

'Wait, we're not finished yet, Sean,' said Ming.

I looked back, and saw Bruce the Spruce picking up a tattoo gun. Laurel was beside him, holding a large pair of pliers.

'I bagsy his toes!' yelled out Loopy Lou. 'I gots to get me one of those!'

'Aw, no fair!' cried Crunchie Haystacks.

'He's gotta throw them like a wedding bouquet!
It's tradition!'

Martin looked up at me, worried, and we both gulped.

'Oh balls.'

# IMAGINARY FRIEND

By Authority of the Corporate League of Imaginary Friends Federation

To Whom It May Concern

On this day... SATURDAY THE 6TH OF NOVEMBER ......in the place of ..JUST OUTSIDE.. BOYLE .in the county of ...ROSCOMMON...in the country of .IRELAND

on the planet of ...THE EARTH.......,

we hereby certify that this person, animal, beast, blob or other weird creature, will henceforth go by the name of ...SEAN "CAUTION" MURPHY

and is hereby licensed to practise as an ...IMAGINARY FRIEND.in accordance with the Laws, Codes and Ideals of Imaginary Friendship as set out in *The Big Massive Manual*, somewhere near the middle.

Hurrah!

Signed by: *Ming the Magpie*

Witnessed by: *Bruce the Spruce*

Second witness: CRUNCHIE HAYSTACKS

IMAGINARY FRIENDS
C.L.I.F.F.

# FIN*

**\*FIN** – A French word meaning 'the end'.
It comes from the time a Frenchman saw a
shark's fin for the first time, and knew it
would be the end of him.

# ABOUT
# CHRIS O'DOWD

Chris O'Dowd is an award-winning actor and writer from the barmy town of Boyle in Ireland. Chris did some good acting in *Bridesmaids*, *The IT Crowd*, *Gulliver's Travels* and *Of Mice and Men*. We won't mention the films where he did bad acting. He has a dog called Potato and a cat who shouts at him for no reason. He studied at University College Dublin and the London Academy of Music and Dramatic Art. He graduated from neither. Chris created *Moone Boy* to get revenge on his sisters for putting make-up on him as a child. He co-wrote the Sky TV series and this book with his good friend Nick Murphy, who is a lot older than Chris.

# ABOUT
# NICK V. MURPHY

Nick V. Murphy is a writer from Kilkenny, Ireland. (The V. in his name stands for Very.) He went to Trinity College Dublin to study English and History, but spent most of his time doing theatre and running away from girls. This was where he bumped into Chris O'Dowd, who was out looking for pizza. After college, Nick focused on writing, which was the laziest career he could think of, as it could even be done while wearing pyjamas. He wrote a few things for TV, then a movie called *Hideaways*, before co-writing a short film with Chris called *Capturing Santa*. The pyjama-wearing pair developed this into the comedy series *Moone Boy*, which recently won an International Emmy for Best Comedy.